A Messy Job
I Never Did See
A Girl Do

A MESSY JOB I NEVER DID SEE A GIRL DO

short stories by

MARY JANE RYALS

6/3/99
For
Barbara —
Best of luck with
your own work —
Best Mary Jane Ryals

Livingston Press

at

The University of West Alabama

ISBN 0-942979-60-5 (cloth)
ISBN 0-942979-59-1 (paper)
Library of Congress # 99-60751

Manufactured in the United States of America

Text layout and design by Jill Wallace
Cover art by Linda Hall, entitled "Home ward"
(consisting of wood, paint, fabric, wheels)
Cover design by Joe Taylor
Manuscript proofreading by Jill Wallace, Stephanie Parnell, Geoffrey Hodge,
Tammy Horn, Stephen Slimp, Kim Smith, and Nicole Green
Printed by Patterson Printing

The author wishes to express thanks to the following publications in which her work originally appeared: *Cold Mountain Review, Connecticut Review, Grab-A-Nickel, Heat, Negative Capability, Oasis, On the Make, Quarter After Eight, Short Story, State Street Review, Yemassee Review.* Some of these stories have also won fiction awards: Florida First Coast Writers' Festival, Hemingway Days Festival, *Negative Capability,* and *Short Story.*

Thanks to the goddesses and gods of fate and the good luck they've handed me so far—food in my mouth every day, beds for my family, a whip-smart son Dylan and a quick-smart daughter Ariel, and a lightning-flash humored man Michael. Thanks for my first readers and encouragers: Michael Trammell, Pat MacEnulty, Barbie Ryals, Pam Ball, Kitty Gretsch, Sheila Ortiz-Taylor, Lizanne Minerva, Donna Decker, Rachelle Smith, and Delores Bryant——all amazing friends who believed when I didn't. Thanks to Dean and Bruce for the computer help. Thanks to Linda Hall for the art. Stephanie Harrell, thanks for the Design Eye. Kitty, thanks for the vision. Thanks also to my wonderful, strong, and droll mother who taught me to love books, to brave most everything, to laugh in the face of dread; and to my creative father who paid for the only material thing he says was worth a damn that he could give me—an education. I would like to remember the late Jerry Stern who taught me the craft of the short story and a lot about how to live and to laugh in the dark. And a huge thanks goes to Joe Taylor who makes it possible.

Thanks also goes to the Florida Arts Council for the yearlong fellowship I received in Tallahassee in 1994-95; also to the Florida Atlantic Center for the Arts for the three-week residency at New Smyrna Beach in 1995; to the National Endowment for the Humanities and the Rockefeller Foundation grant and three-week residency in Chicago in 1995 and a two-week stay at the Hambridge Center in Dillard, Georgia, in 1998. These monies, the time and space provided, and the people who make it all possible for artists to work, helped me tremendously.

Livingston Press specializes in offbeat and/or Southern literature. For a catalogue, please write us at Station 22, University of West Alabama, Livingston, AL 35470.

CONTENTS

To Ariel, Dylan and Michael

AT THE OTHER END OF NOWHERE

I tell my toss-and-roll stomach and then my Aunt Bebe it's just a plastic flipper with a strap for a heel, the kind that goes with fins and snorkel, stuck in the chain-link fence by the nearly crimson and flooded St. Mark's River. Just a plastic nothing flipper flung and stuck by the flood. I walk out of the still mucky Posey's Oyster Bar that I live in the second story of and pull the nothing flipper out with a thwack to show her, since I have one silver-film eye and one regular. The silver eye helps me see things others do not. But the flood spell has already crept upon my aunt, and I can see by her face that the shadow of things burns in her, my mama Meredith's pretty sister, Aunt Bebe.

Uncle Bucky says the big company that stores their oil down here donated the orange barge. Down here where the St. Marks River and the Wakulla River meet then empty out into the Gulf of Mexico. The orange barge the National Guard and the Red Cross got onto to get Aunt Bebe and me and other people with skiffs to help out. Uncle Bucky said the barge and all the boats it dragged with it drifted past the deck on the water, past the dance floor, past the restaurant and bar, alongside our big house and bar with my Aunt Bebe's flat-bottom skiff. We drifted right past the house and bar on into the flooded street. I do not remember that part so I can not swear to it. Uncle Bucky had stood on the roof of the second story of Posey's because the beds, sofa, stereo, clothes and trash from mine and Mama's house was now knee-deep in floodwater on the second floor. Uncle Bucky said first he thought God had parted the river and a wall of broil and growl flood river would swallow him. When it did not, he took it as a warning of the news to come. He said the river broiled and growled like it was being seared from above, and Aunt Bebe said the way the flood spit and fumed and gushed and stunk under us on the barge, it looked like we would bust into Posey's and that only hers and everybody else's will kept it back and floated us all onto River Road. Into River Road where a flat-bottomed, no-motored boat cast mullet nets over the street where fish leapt and splished, caught in a trap at the other end of nowhere, what my mama called Posey's Oyster Bar at St. Marks, the confluence of two rivers that feed the gulf. I would never eat those light-bellied mullet though. Some lay stacked up on the roof of the restaurant across the street, one eye facing us and silver-skinned, drowning in the air, flood-diseased.

Used to be, when men thick from eating big would come into the tile floor, fluorescent lit and split log tabled Posey's Oyster Bar and say, "Where's this we're at?" Mama in her burlap apron would say, "At the other end of nowhere. Come on in and try the oysters." My half-Seminole brown mama in her tennis shoes she'd painted sea apple green. I would ice down the beer and wrap paper plates of shrimp with plastic to zap in the microwave for later customers while the men with thick waists from eating big would slort down oysters and say, "I tried to get my old lady to do that" and "Try piano wire" and then "I like a g-string myself," and then they'd laugh with a broil and growl. Mama would walk and twist her way through them all and give her new nickel smile for tip money to pay the mortgage on Posey's Oyster Bar at the other end of nowhere. Sometimes I would bring them the sauce with green and red peppers that wrung salt water from their eyes. They'd sniffle and say, "Boy! What's in this damn sauce—your eye?" and they'd laugh. But those thick men did not know about my special sight, and laughed with a broil and a growl at their joke about my eye in their sauce.

I could see with my silver-film eye how my mama turned into a mermaid weekend nights when the other end of nowhere Posey's Oyster Bar got so sardined with people, when the Karaoke machine and the band called Little Rock came on, nights it could take twenty minutes to get from the front screen door, past the bar, past the dollar bills taped to the wall that said "Blue is Blood" and "Get off Jewels," and "Light my Skiff." Then past the bathrooms, past the juke box to the concrete dance floor and Karaoke machine. Around nine, when the sky turned from chalk to black, my mama and the other two waitresses all sang "Blue Eyes Crying in the Rain" or "She Talks to Angels." That's when I saw it happen. From Mama's sea apple tennis shoes to her tight-jeans legs up to her just-under-the-bellybutton, she turned to fish fins and sea apple green scales that glittered like moonlight on the river out past the dance floor by the deck. Her naked breasts turned to jars of garden flesh and her face flashed ruby and twilit.

Then the men changed. Not the thick from eating men, but the skin-and-bones with leather skin men who spent their days with gulf waves slapping their boat sides while they fished the wiggle and squirm mullet from the bay. From under the bar by the deck next to the concrete dance floor, with my silver-film eye I had watched these men turned after dark to seahorses with curled back feet and spiny skin. They had nodded their arched necks like sea-wave love to the rhythm of the mermaids' songs. Songs of wet highways, songs of the moon shining through the water like champagne, songs of the people from the south wind, songs of how the dolphins still know, songs with lines something like "I ain't a-feared of dying, it's just the thought of you being gone." Songs blue as Spain. My mama, the queen of all mermaids at night, the saddest of women at the other end of nowhere, whose lover, my daddy, she had told me, had finally fallen into the bottom of the bottle for good.

When we got back to Posey's Oyster Bar that day after being towed by the orange barge, Aunt Bebe let Uncle Bucky scrape her skiff onto dry land. When his rescuing arms reached up to pull her out of the boat that had steered the death-guiding currents, she only disbelieved him for a minute, hesitating like he might be bait. Then she reached out for his whalish arms and he lifted her down onto real ground. Then I fell into his arms like prairies of long water. Aunt Bebe would not look back at her boat, like a person who goes to a funeral burial and turns their head away when the casket is dropped, the dirt spilling onto its top. Like they can't bear more so they turn away, their face creased in a deeper sense of the wreck to come.

My Aunt Bebe says when the barge dropped her and me and her boat way up the St. Marks River, she thought they'd made a mistake, steered her into the gulf. The water, she says, broiled and roared red and stank, and green plastic garbage pails roiled by. I do not talk about it because I do not remember. Aunt Bebe says in that night all you could see was the pink light on the barge's bow and the broil and roar of the floodwaters, the humming under it like blood as it sliced and dissolved the face of this earth.

Aunt Bebe said she and I all that night drove in dream-sweat her boat over the broil and roar of waters, wondering why the men on the barge had put us way out into the Gulf. Until we heard desire's restless breath in the branches of a tree, and when she shined her floodlight on it in the distance, we saw golden eyes, jewels, winking pearls, a universe of sea and stars. When Aunt Bebe drove her boat over to the tree, she saw it was the A-frame of a tool shed in the floodwaters and the silver and jewels and winking pearls. But then the universe of sea and stars were the eyes of lizards and snakes, and the wings of flying roaches, piled writhes of life stuck on the roof. My aunt says the lizards and snakes and the flying roaches flung their bodies from the rooftop into the flue-black water or into the gun-blue sky so they could swim or fly to the boat, but instead they were spun and shoved into the stench waters washing away. She says after that, we got careful about trees and were not fooled again by their gold-jeweled and pearl-winking eyes, their universe of sea and stars. I do not know because I do not remember.

Aunt Bebe said when the morning came, the sun did not seem to come up, but the rain spit and showered and the rocks in the river shook loose from thunder. We had to gobble in air under hands umbrellaed over our mouths. That's when the young deer with long legs floated by backwards. The way it floated by backwards, the way it floated past, its head only poked out of the water holding up stubs for antlers, Aunt Bebe said it looked like a big brown porpoise coming up for air, with that same spit and gasp. But convulsing over and over, not spit-gasping and then diving below. Aunt Bebe said she lassoed the stubs of deer antler with an anchor rope and tried to pull him in, but it did not work so good because the head dipped lower and the two blow holes started to not spit-gasp but to gurgle out water in pools and its velveteen head began to disappear, like a too-heavy anchor at the end of the rope. So she cut it off. When I asked Aunt Bebe, "What was that?" she said it was nothing. Just nothing. She cut the rope and set out over the broil and roar.

At high noon, the sky melted down to a muddied seagull gray. Still no sun. That's when Aunt Bebe says she spied the black baby on a ski rope. She said it looked like somebody had tied a strong nylon rope about that baby's waist and still held on, since the other end sunk straight down into the waters. That baby tore through the current, arms and head up and back like it had broken the surface to do a back flip back into the water that it was still taking and taking and taking, but nothing came or went. My Aunt Bebe said when she got up close and pulled the yellow ski rope from where it sunk straight down, it felt too light

for a hang-on anchor. She said it gave like it was letting go or being let
go of.

When Aunt Bebe pulled back over to the orange barge, she says the
pink light bled all in the water, and those Red Cross and National Guard
men on the barge pulled us up and handed her a Budweiser and a leg of
fried chicken and stacked the black baby up with the rest. She said they
asked about my eye, and they could not get me to eat chicken or drink
Coke for singing the songs my Mama loved and sang when she turned
sea apple green and scaly jeweled from just under the belly button down.
I sang "Blue Eyes Crying in the Rain" and "She Talks to Angels."

My Aunt Bebe said when we got back out on the sewer-yellow
water in the dim-star night, that's when she first saw the green apple
tennis shoe stuck on the barb wire fence first. Then the other one bob-
bing like it got uprooted. Aunt Bebe said Mama's skin did not come off
when she tried to lift her body, blowing like a sail in the torrents of
water and rain, like some other people's did. Aunt Bebe says I told her
that's because Mama decided to be a mermaid full time now. But I do
not know because I do not remember. Aunt Bebe said Mama's stomach
faced the waters and her right arm sleeve was stuck on the barbed wire
over her head, and her face turned sideways towards us like she had
been swimming away away away from the broil and groan with the
humming under it like blood as it sliced and dissolved the face of this
earth. Aunt Bebe says she yelled "Come on, Meredith, swim! Swim!"
as she drove the boat over to her. She says that when she unstuck Mama's
sea apple green tennis shoes and unstuck her shirt, even then Aunt Bebe
talked to her, saying, "Meredith, it's gonna be all right now, it's gonna
be all right." She held my mama's broiled body in her arms and did not
look at her face but at the place on her arm that seemed to have a big
bug bite that did not bleed because all the blood had been broiled and
growled out of her. The men on the barge stepped down into the boat
where Aunt Bebe held my mama and I sang "Blue Eyes Crying in the
Rain" and I hugged myself and they hefted us up onto the barge and

laid Mama's body stacked on top of the black baby's body, like the rest of the broiled out bodies, stacked them like they were stacking fried mullet at a fish fry.

At dawn three days later, when the crows turned white and cawed overhead, my Aunt Bebe says that barge got full. The men headed the barge back down the swelled river, and even though they would see things, things that caught their eye in a peacock feather way stuck in the firs and fences and roofs of buildings, they did not stop. They would not stop. They could not stop. Boats like my aunt's were stacked on the barge and they sprayed the people with embalming fluid, the people stacked like mullet on the barge and covered them with dull green tarp. Lots of men, the ones who turned into seahorses when my mama had sung to the Karaoke machine, stood around not looking at the tarp and stood not looking at their skiffs they'd used to bring back bodies. They stared into the broil and growl water as if waiting for broiled faces to bob up as if to say hello one last time before going back under. Aunt Bebe says we all looked out at the tops of trees and fences and roofs along the St. Mark's River that had snagged the broiled up people. The stench of decay hung around like gin, after somebody's been drinking all night. I do not know, because I do not remember anything except my mama's sea apple green tennis shoes. Those people stood looking hard as bones, because they knew back home they'd never be able to broil a red snapper or look at a piece of nothing caught in the barbed wire ever the same again, even when I could see it with my silver-filmed eye, pull it out of the fence to show them it was just a piece of nothing flipper thrown up by the wind. And me, I knew my mama was a mermaid then, hired on full time permanent under the ocean and free.

PIG ON A STICK

Me and Sister and Olivette lie in our big bed at night waiting for the wild hog with hairs on its back to come rooting under the house. He snorts over to the place in the floor that's caved in and we see his gleaming eye pink as a slapped face or a raised up scar on your leg. When he butts, the house shakes terrible.

Olivette whimpers and I do not wallop her since she's three. I am eleven now. Sister, who Mama thought would be the baby, is not the baby. She's eight and tearful. By eight, you ought to know to buck up. I want to slap the skin off her.

All our stomachs twist up from no food since Mama and Daddy left a week ago. Yesterday breakfast we ate the last of the black bananas Mama stashed in the freezer to make banana bread. Sister's always been hateful. I turned three when Sister started crawling and stuffing live roaches and filthy socks in her mouth. One day I forgot to watch her. She toppled on down the concrete front steps and busted her mouth. Mama yelled so loud at me it rang through the sewage pipes. That's when I asked Mama when would we be taking Sister back to the hospital where she came from. Mama clobbered me good with a right knuckle full.

So I smooshed Sister in a bucket and hauled her down to Jerusalem Road to see if any colored people wanted to buy her. They did not. So I says to myself, Juney Mae, buck up. That's what I said on the way home, sweating up the hill with that Sister in a bucket.

People say the reason Mama's left us to travel with the Mexican woman who walked tightrope in that coming-through-town circus is cause we live on Fagg Street, two g's on the fagg. Seven days ago, Mama pulled on her tutu with her stomach bulging out towards Russia. Then she pulled down all the milk glass from the kitchen shelf, laid it on the floor, then let the pull take her body out the house.

Daddy had meant to fix the floor two years ago. When their fights started. The floor fixing argument turned into one of those fights I call foundational between them. Finally, Daddy drove home from his bread route which sprawled from Bainbridge, Georgia to Mayo, Florida, and Mama informed him she didn't love his fat ass no more.

You might say she said it cause she possessed the eight-month pregnant rages, but this time her voice rang it up loud through the pipes and pronounced it like they do a school announcement, over the intercom. Into the commode. Mama always goes for love.

After Mama left, Daddy took to the road. The colored folk think he went down to the Marine Corps office and signed up to go kill those Viet Congs.

The pig huffs and snorts under the house like it's already got shot and is lying waiting for the rotisserie. I swear I smell bacon frying, but then all I hear is horny hog breath through those snout holes.

"It's a ghost," Sister whines. "See those pink eyes?"

"It ain't, neither," I says. "It's a damn wild hog, fool."

"I'm scared," she says. "What if that one-eyed wolf comes and kills it? What if the wolf bites us?"

She'd heard a story from some white trash boy she sits with on the school bus. Buck teeth boy harboring only eight toes and courts her with scary stories. Told her a one-eyed wolf lives in the swamp down our road. Bites another wolf and that wolf grows four eyes and that wolf bites another wolf and that wolf grows eight eyes and so on. I settle for wild hogs. They say wild hogs are really farm pigs that escaped and roam where they please. All I know is, they're mean and strong.

Olivette climbs up into my lap on the bed, smelling like yeast rising. We watch the Cartwrights on *Bonanza* and eat a great feast of chicken legs and whatall. Daddy got a brand new RCA TV, in color, on his last pay day. Mama had screamed What about the utilities bill. If it rains real hard, the heavy TV might just crash on through the floor. I do not know how we'll get some groceries, either.

Sister whimpers herself on to sleep. I watch the avocado sky, monsoon summer. Olivette breathes sweet and sticky three-year-old breath on my neck. Pop Tarts, grapes, sticky buns. Groceries. My stomach rumbles as the hog roots its horns at the concrete blocks under the house, and our bed shakes like some devil got hold of it. The house rumbles and so does my stomach.

Olivette doesn't look like me and Sister—her hair squash yellow, wheaty freckles and blackberry eyes. Me and Sister got chocolate hair and cat green eyes. Olivette doesn't look like daddy, neither. But that's another story I don't know nothing about. Olivette I took to be my baby cause Mama didn't have time for her. Three years ago, when Mama bulged out big with Olivette, I pretended I bulged out at the stomach and told the colored boy J.C. down at Jerusalem Road I would be delivering soon. Real soon.

He had spoiled it all by telling his mama. She had told him it would be a modern miracle if an eight-year-old girl gave birth. So I fisted him in the nose and he run home with a snotty beige and rosy bleeding nose. Fixed him.

This morning, before the hail heavy rain of July, here comes Aunt Beauty running her car up the drive in a big skinny speed. Possum carcass squished into the grill of her old Studebaker, lawn mower sticking out the trunk. I wonder how I can boil this greasy possum. I heard the colored people eats possum, and so why can't we?

Here she comes, zooming up our driveway where the runoff from summer storms is carving out ragged ditches and hollowed out cave-like holes in the clay. Bottle of Southern Comfort in her left hand and gear shifting with her right. Rifle in the seat beside her like always.

To say "old" Studebaker is white-lying. To Aunt Beauty, car driving is an experiment, a hot off the griddle activity. Aunt Beauty'd always rode a horse till a year before when she surrendered it up. They finally outlawed horse riding in town. Aunt Beauty didn't like not having a way to get around, and she got herself into extra trouble drinking behind McCrory's one night and going to pee on the steps of the state capitol across the street.

The police threatened to arrest her for the seventh time. The on-duty officer shook his head and said "Beauty, Beauty." Patient and each word like a preacher on Wednesday night prayer meeting. "With all due respect, Beauty." That is all he had to say.

She got herself a driver's license up in Georgia. I still don't understand the math of it. Took her less than six months to get her license revoked in Georgia for a ten year period. Refused to go to the license bureau and get a Florida one.

"Anybody called me yet?" she says, getting out of the Studebaker. The turquoise phone Mama picked out has a cord to match, perched on the living room tea table next to the settee. Mama has high falutin' ideas concerning interior decor. Immediately, our house converts into Aunt Beauty's personal telephone booth. Aunt Beauty's always thought of our house as her movie star dressing room.

I start the water to boiling and saw off the possum's head. I use a kitchen knife to saw the tissue between its hairy skin from the muscle.

I only retch once.

Aunt Beauty possesses the pure ugliness of a barn rat. She's learned some talent with the men, though. She wiles away this afternoon's heavy rain laying around on the sofa calling various and sundry boyfriends while me and Sister and Olivette chew possum meat. Aunt Beauty's boiling up who she might coax into slipping her pool-table quarters and Miller High Life six-packs for going out tonight.

She's brought the lawn mower, she says, to mow the back field. But the lawn mower's got a broken part, she says.

"Field needs cutting down, Juney, it's big as you," she claims. Which, I want to say, ain't tall at all, four foot ten, but something to brag about if you're yellow-beige grass and weeds hanging in the wind. I suddenly picture a pineapple upside down cake with pure white sugar and pecans and butter. I'm still hungry.

When the hushing ambush of the evening falls down around us, Aunt Beauty leaves out the front door with a stand-around dress, mail-ordered. Says, Y'all be good and don't let the wild boar get you. Sister whines and Olivette sits up in my lap. TV on. We watch *Twilight Zone* and whatall and wait to hear the Studebaker growl up the drive and cough to a stop. It never does.

But some foxes come around up under the house and growl and scrap with the wild boar. Sister cries blue tears into the bedspread where the chenille's wore off. I suggest we steal some old rooster with no balls or wring a hen's neck down on Jerusalem Road and swindle some eggs. Sister cries louder. Peanut butter's gone, I remind her. I want to snap her head off. The hog's squealing louder than a truck under the house.

Then Sister does it. Reaches down and touches the hairy hog. She takes in a breath like she seen god or took communion with Catholics chomping a big chunk of bread and sharp taste of wine in a silver cup. Makes me mad as fire. I wanted to touch that ridiculous pig first, eyes like a fish just before dying.

I could eat hog eyes on toast. My stomach's twisty again. That hog does not even notice her touch, still squealing as the foxes bully it. I take a large satisfaction in this.

In the morning I threaten to wallop Olivette and Sister so hard they'll fly across the room if they say so much as one syllable about no sweet jam and toast. Sister's put me in a foul mood, suggesting how fatty and sweet Olivette's meat would be if we cooked her up. My skin's getting tighter over my swollen mad as a bullet self.

This is when Aunt Beauty brings home a biker.

"Name's Baldy," he says, holding out his knuckles hairy as garlic roots. He's got three tattoos I can see, multi-colored. Key lime pie green anchor on his forearm. Watermelon red "Mom" over his heart. Chicken-vein blue "In God We Trust" on his neck. He will fix the lawn mower, he says, stumbling through tall weeds, wading through backyard stickers to the empty chicken house.

For light out in the chicken house, he's rigged a flashlight that begins to glow faded. Olivette and me hang around out there. She crawls and walks and wanders around, and I try to stop her from chewing on old chicken turds and stale corn.

After a six-pack of Anheuser Busch, Baldy falls upon a greater idea than food, he says, finer than just a loaf of Wonder Bread. Baldy has a plan. He takes my bicycle and rigs up the lawn mower motor to the back wheel, gears and bike chains grinding like a buzz saw. Sister practices cartwheels in the front yard with J.C. who she calls Jacob. I get her to watch Olivette so I can test drive the motor bike. It has one speed only: haul ass or die.

Besides Baldy, Aunt Beauty has also brought home six tins of smoked oysters and a dead rabbit. She skins this rabbit and hands it over to me to cook.

We eat stewed chewy rabbit dinner and oysters for dessert. They stick to our teeth. Still hungry, we lick the stick off our teeth.

Aunt Beauty takes out her pistol. We all follow her outside into a skunk black night. She fires at the old oak tree by the darker woods. Blam Blam Blam, its leaves shaking and shimmying like a riot of locusts until Aunt Beauty runs out of rounds.

"Baldy, I'm bored," she says, and he lights her up a Lucky Strike. They decide to drive on down to the Panacea dump near the coast and shoot big rats. Olivette and Sister and me watch the Studebaker taillights jitter like rattles on a snake. They wind down the ditchy road.

Next day, Aunt Beauty sleeps on the velveteen sofa all day, waking only for an occasional kiss on the you-know-where from Baldy. Me and Olivette and Sister don't care cause they brought home potatoes and a plain rectangle of plywood with the word "Jesus" painted in cherry red letters.

Olivette and me change our Barbie doll's outfit from the wedding dress to the ball gown to the ballerina costume to the cowgirl skirt in the dirt of our front yard. Sister's off playing with that J.C. colored boy again. I set out on the chicken barn motor bike, haul ass speed down Fagg Street. Flying on down to Jerusalem Road by the swamp. I find her and J.C. in the bushes showing each other their equipment.

"Sister, what you doing showing J.C. your privatecy?" I says. She starts wailing and says he brought her a plate of fried mullet and collards and cheese grits as a trade for a looksee, and I wallop her. I turn to tell J.C. to get out of my face but he's disappeared.

I put Sister on the bike basket and we have one wreck on the way home where Sister smashes her face into the dirt road and cries again. I swear to the Lord I am about to bust from inside I'm so mad. Mad as a pig on a stick. I make her walk the rest of the way cause she's a fat ass, I tell her. Her face is a spectacle with tears and blood and clay mixed together. I enjoy the speed on this motor bicycle as I pass her by.

Aunt Beauty cooks potatoes and somewhere she's acquired butter and cheese to melt on top. After that, Baldy teaches me and Sister to smoke Lucky Strikes. Aunt Beauty shows us some tumbling tricks on the velveteen sofa. She stands on her head and drinks from her gin bottle. Baldy cheers and says he's amazed, and she could make some cash monies doing that for the circus.

That sets Sister off and she cries for Mama. And Daddy. Aunt Beauty hands her the gun and the gin bottle and tells her things aren't so bad. They go outside and shoot off some rounds while me and Baldy go to the barn and rig up a cart and nail the "Jesus" sign on the back. We'll go down to Jerusalem Road and offer rides to colored people for a dime or for some corn and tomatoes.

But the next week brings the tall unmowed grass dry and rattly and Baldy chops Aunt Beauty across the jaw. She pulls the gun on him and he leaves. I take the haul-ass speed motor bicycle down to Jerusalem Road but the colored kids look at me like I'm crazy. I figure I need to set an example, so I go ask to borrow a pig from J.C.'s mama. I put that pig in the back of the cart and ride around, the pig squealing, sitting straight up.

How in this world am I supposed to know it will kill a pig to sit it up like that so it can't get its circulation going?

"What you trying to prove?" J.C.'s mama asks when I drive that slumped over pig back to her.

"I don't know," I say. "But I'll trade you this high speed bicycle for a slab of this pig." She calls me a foolish white trash girl and I'm so mad I just speed away with the pig, J.C.'s mama hollering at me all down the street.

Aunt Beauty goes to town with Olivette and Sister and somehow returns with Hostess Twinkies and Jell-O and fruit cocktail in a can. She hangs up the pig, slits it down the middle, skins it, guts it and starts drinking early saying men are a sorry lot. She's chopping the pig into parts and I cannot watch this so I step inside and witness one of the TV stories, *The Love of Life*. I boil a whole pile of ribs in the black kettle out back. We eat a grand feast of pork and Hostess Twinkies and mold green Jell-O with canned fruit.

Aunt Beauty leaves early and the wild hog comes up under the house. We are no longer scared of him. For fun, I suggest to Sister that we burn the hairs off his back with matches Baldy left. We torch his hairs and soon he's squealing mad and starts butting at the concrete blocks. Butting and butting and butting and he won't stop squealing and the house rumbles from way down deep like a million ghosts live right under this earth.

Sister and me and Olivette all hang on to one another and wait. That pig just loses his mind, bashing and beating and blundering his head under the rumbling house, and then it happens.

A moan like a tree falling over comes out of the house. We fall off the bed, flung into the front corner wall squealing, and the wild hog's squealing too as he hauls ass out into the fields. Escaped squealing again. The whole floor falls out of the bedroom. Then we hear the other side of the house fall sideways and furniture and whatall slamming up against the wall. We sit in the corner all night. Sister sleeps. Olivette climbs into my lap and my nose stings, she feels so trusty and sweet. She still believes our mama will come home. My nose stings so bad it's like when you snort a bunch of bath water up your snout and think you'll drown. I tell myself, *Juney, buck up.* My nose stops stinging and I think of what I'll do because Olivette *is* my baby now.

I'll take the mattress out into the back field where the tall weeds and grasses rustle about. We'll get some sun on our legs and sleep under the stars. We'll get by. We'll get food some way or the other. We'll make our home in the tall dry grass and weeds. This rightens me and I doze.

Next morning we climb out of the house and drag the mattress out back. I find an old jar of honey, crystallized. I'll have to bust it open so we can suck on hard honey. We start playing up under the mimosa tree. Its fronds sparkle with diamond raindrops and I think of alligators covered in jewels. Up comes Aunt Beauty with two plastic Halloween masks and nylon costumes. Me and Sister fight over the princess one cause the other one's a pig. The blue lace princess gown rips, so Sister puts on the mask. Olivette puts on the pig costume. Aunt Beauty carries a scythe and she's drunk. I glance back at our house that looks like it's on its knees in prayer. I think of meatballs, donuts, a bag of Cheetos.

"Come on, Juney," Aunt Beauty says, looking at the jar of hard white honey in my hand, waving the scythe. "It's time we got things in order," she says. "Let's go cut the grass out back."

I hold the honey jar, staring at the back of her head as she walks with the scythe out to the tall dry grass and weeds.

SATURDAY STREET

"Where that doll come from?" Cookie says. She's wearing her kitchen-yellow Sunday dress with the matching socks and lace and black patent leather shoes. Looks mighty good on her mahogany skin. I been waiting here in our hideout for her to get out of church.

"I brought it from home," I say, stroking the doll's black yarn hair. My greatgrandma gave me the doll made with a rick-rack Seminole skirt crow-black and pumpkin and water-blue colored. She called it a love doll. She said she made it for me to remind me that I do not hate my mama, I just haven't learned to love her.

"You still play with dolls?" Cookie says. "You eleven years old, girl."

My nerves are gnarled up like a cocoon. "Leave me alone," I say, hugging the doll. Today I been thinking about my mama locked up in the hospital for being schizo. And I can't let anybody white find out my best friend is a colored girl. Those people in town and my daddy, too, say coloreds wouldn't want to go to the movies or swim in white pools if the outsiders, the communists, hadn't put it in their heads.

Cookie shrugs and holds out the transistor radio she's swiped from her Aunt Jesse's closet. I show her the gold glittery high heels and the peeking-out-toes high heels I've stolen from Mama's closet. Cookie slips on the gold slippers and I get the ones where my toes show. We feel cool in summer heat listening to transistor radio music on WTAL AM.

When Cookie swishes her hips back and forth and sings "Love Potion Number Nine" and "Rescue Me," her calves stretch and strain pretty in those powerful-as-morning-glories high heels. She dances around holding her nose and singing that she didn't know her days from nights and how she was gonna kiss just about everything in her sights.

Cookie twitches in Mama's gold shoes and sings the words to "Rescue Me," loud and beautiful as a wild orchid high in a palm tree with Mama's gold shoes.

But today I have sweat on the insides of my knees and I feel some change coming. I stand wobbly on the peekaboo toes high heels, holding my doll.

"I wish you would hush up," I say. A bird in the bush nearby twitches, nervous with us around. Cookie stops, stands tall and stares me down. Her brown arms on her hips and her towering six whole inches over me, her mouth tight, as if she's wondering if she ought to clobber me.

She steps out of the gold shoes that smell of musty closet and she says "Trade me back."

I act like my mama when she's only half crazy and doesn't approve of my using a soup spoon at the table when I'm supposed to use a teaspoon.

Then I prance upon an idea. "I want to take a walk down Saturday Street," I say. In my magic gold shoes, I don't say aloud, to see your brother with eyes like Brazil and skin like bittersweet chocolate; Ivory Jones is his name. We could juke by Johnny's house where Ivory Jones and Johnny stay sometimes in the afternoons.

"Yeah!" she says. I pull off the peekaboo heels and she hands over my gold slippers with the Kleenex to stuff the toes. Cookie's feet will hold the toe-peek shoes with no stuffing in the heels.

We clomp down the dirt road that cuts through the swamp of screamy green lily pads and paper white flowers. We pass purple thistles in the brush by the road, the bullfrogs chugging lazy and low. My love doll's arm I don't hold drags in the dirt road. I smell the damp earth of rotting things and my toes start to ache as we turn onto Saturday Street.

The road dusts up dirt and the houses sit small, painted bright as a wheelbarrow full of flowers—bright blue or red or yellow. The pit of my stomach claws at me. I've never been where so many colored people live and only me white. What if they decide to snatch me away?

Cookie takes my arm with her hand as we stand at the end of the street. "I hope Voodoo Lady ain't home," she says.

"Who?" I say, my word trembling into two.

"Voodoo Lady," she says pointing down to the scarlet fever red house down about the middle of the rutted street. "She real skinny and bushy haired. Look like a Q-tip that done blew up," she says. "One time she done went over to the post office. Held those gourds of hers like they was Aaron's rod, holding them gourds up over her shoulders, shaking them so they rattle like a snake. And when the postman say Can I help you she say 'No, you got evil thoughts in you head.'"

Cookie's let go my arm and I admire the blue black on the outer edge of her colored girl mouth as she finishes her story. "So she goes to the other guy and she shakes them gourds at him; he laughs at her; then, half hour later, he doubled over with the stomach ache and flat on his back at the hospital. Pendicitis."

"Well, let's go on home, then," I say, turning and pulling like a mule on her arm.

"Come on, don't be a chicken liver," Cookie says, yanking me the other way. I let her take us clomping down Saturday Street, me in shorts holding my doll to protect me, her in Sunday kitchen yellow clothes. We walk wibbly wobbly down the dusty dirt street until we get to Johnny's house. Two stories high, red brick, bigger than the wooden and block ones on either side. Johnny and Ivory Jones scrub circles of bubbles like clouds on Johnny's daddy's bird egg blue Valiant.

"Hooo, girl," Johnny says. He's fifteen and cute his own self. He can not take his eyes off Cookie. I get a shock knowing that my boobies haven't even pushed out to chocolate kisses yet, hers already like ice cream licked down some in the cones. "Girl, take me to heaven," he says. Ivory Jones stares at me up and down cool as Alaska with his eyes like Brazil and I get a weak-kneed and tee-tottering feeling come over me.

"What y'all doing down here?" Ivory Jones says. His arm muscles look carved and skin smooth like your mama's nightgown. But a wrinkled up frown looks stern as a daddy.

"You ain't my boss, boy," Cookie says to Ivory Jones. Johnny laughs.

"Your sister womanish," Johnny says. Cookie told me before that means a sassy colored girl.

"Come on over and help us foam up this car," Johnny says. Ivory Jones does not like that, by the way his Brazil-eyes half close, and that makes my stomach do the twist. Cookie grabs me by the hand and we wobble up the driveway.

"I'm going to be a singer in Chicago," Cookie says to Johnny. "Want to hear me sing?" He says sure and she breaks out into "Baby Baby Sweet Baby." Singing and swaying, she forgets where we are. I close my eyes and wonder where the world goes. All I know is Cookie's low alto. I squash my love doll in the back waistband of my shorts where I sweat like a flying bird does not.

Ivory Jones ignores his sister Cookie, washing the car as Johnny leans up against a tree fold-armed eyeing Cookie's twitching hips. When she finishes, Johnny claps and Cookie bows low in her kitchen yellow dress and Johnny says something I don't quite understand, something about how about giving him something, I'm not sure what.

Ivory Jones stands up straight and squeezes out his sponge and says to me, "Your Mama know you got them shoes?" I shake my head no and hug my doll. "They dangerous," he says, glancing back at Johnny and Cookie.

"Come over here, girl, and show me," Johnny says to Cookie and Cookie walks closer to him.

"Johnny," Ivory Jones says, dropping the sponge.

"Come on over here, tall girl," Johnny says, ignoring Ivory Jones. Cookie walks up to him close enough to spit. He leans over and starts to kiss her. They give a big mouth kiss like sucking a Tootsie Roll Pop, the whole thing in your mouth and your tongue circling it. Ivory Jones makes big to little cloud circles, storm clouds and tornadoes in suds on the car.

Everything is waiting inside me. Everything is waiting to explode like Easter Sunday at church during *Gloria in Excelsis* when the brass instruments play and they have toted in the special palm trees for decorations in the front of the church.

But then I think of the moon with its one yellow eye, the moon of Brazil, the Voodoo Lady. Then something inside me bites hard and I know when this kiss happens for the first time, something will vanish, will leap out. I'd have to think a bunch of moons over that. If I kissed Ivory Jones' blueberry pie lips it might start to happen, running all over and through and down my legs like blood, so I reach around and grab my doll, squeeze her so hard I can feel my fingers meet my thumb between her front and back.

Out comes the Voodoo Lady from her scarlet fever red house next door hollering and shaking her gourds. "Take you crazy girl baby out of here and wash that car on the street before I hexes on you. Get the girl baby," she says and she's swinging a chicken's foot tied with red string over her head. There's a cross chalked on her front door in pajama blue. Every word she says is nonsense, and I understand every bit of it.

Oh, lord, somebody says, and I think about last time they took Mama to the hospital after she covered the windows to shut out the children screaming because she said their legs and arms got blown off in a country called Laos. A week later the tainted truth of it had come over the radio news, and Mama in a psycho-bed on the 5C ward of the hospital where Daddy is the administrator.

"Get the girl baby," the Voodoo Lady is saying. I back down the driveway, hugging my doll to my chest.

"Now look at the trouble you done caused," Ivory Jones says to Cookie who's stopped kissing Johnny and looks over at me in a summer-hazy way.

"Come on back here, girl," she says. "Chicken liver baby."

I run out the drive way and clomp my hurting toes down the dirt road of Saturday Street hearing Ivory Jones' voice lilting across the swamp, using his big brother voice on Cookie, saying "Aunt Jesse gonna get you."

"No, she ain't. She can't do nothing but whip me and only if she catch me," Cookie says.

But I am running. I run past the Saturday Street stop sign and do not stop, run past the rotting damp smell of earth, run past the stand-out purple thistles, run past the bullfrogs, run past the lily pads, and one of my shoes flips off, and I fall and skin my knee and tear my doll's dress.

I get up grunting tears, my bloody muddy knee. I don't look back at the shoe and I hobble fast up the rocky slick road of clay, past Jesse's and Cookie's and Ivory Jones' driveway with that one high heel pinching my toes. I come down hard on the rocky road with the gold heel smeared in mud now, so I shake that shoe off and don't look back and I keep running.

When I get to our hideout, I cry blue-skinned beetle tears into my love doll's stomach. I want Ivory Jones and me to be two halves of an orange, a highway that goes both ways, I want two shoes that fit. Holding my love doll tight, tight, tight, thinking about Cookie kissing Johnny for the longest minute in the world, when here she comes holding my broken gold shoe and singing that she was going to kiss everything in sight. I take that shoe back and look at her and for no reason at all we both start laughing like water running down the creek between our two houses.

A MESSY JOB I NEVER DID SEE A GIRL DO

In the black-as-boots night I can hear Loki below and next door whinny, stamp, back jam and kick to get out of the tall-ceilinged red barn. The crickets bree and an owl who-who's after early summer rain licks the earth and air.

During the storm we get every summer night, my daddy's white knuckled fist snapped across Mama's jaw after she called him a white trash drunk she should've not married. My boiling stomach had urged me on and I screamed "Y'all knock it off," even though Daddy or Mama could have come down the hall to rattle and shake me out of the bed or slam my head up against the wall like Mama's head went against the TV once. Instead they get after-violent quiet. Daddy's gun case in the hallway separates me from their room. Gun case holding the flintlock musket, Kentucky percussion rifle, the Winchester and Derringer and the shotgun Daddy uses for deer hunting.

But now it's Loki restless, a stud without a mare and quick cooking underneath. Tomorrow I will pull a curry comb through his mane and tail, a body brush over his Thoroughbreded sleekness and try to ride him. He's black as the ivory-inlaid table Daddy brought back from the Korea war he still does not talk about twelve years later.

Daddy's fury jumps contagious all into Mama's bones. If I sass her about not feeding fighting chickens that claw your arms, she will find a Weeping Willow switch and whrip whrip on my legs.

Mama and Daddy run the Ratskeller Hunting Club that gets held meetings here every Saturday night. The men drink bottles of Jack and bet on chicken fights; the women cook in the back of the barn with a hose-down kitchen where kids with dirty fingernails teach each other poker tricks.

My daddy just fell on the idea of keeping Loki and breeding him. The Ratskeller Hunting Club keeps this young horse in the church-high barn where Christmas lights hang strung from rafters and the men play chicken fight gambling.

The only light Loki can see comes in when lightnings flash at night where the tin broken roof is replaced by green plastic. Loki, I believe, feels under water.

In the morning I get up and walk to the walnut panel kitchen and see Mama has Avon-Ladied "Blushing Beige" on the bruise of her left cheek. Tonight, Saturday chicken and card game night, Mama wants to make an impression on the women.

"Don't go thinking you're going to ride that horse today," she says, taking twelve frozen Supreme white bread loaves out of the freezer. "You've got to help me make tuna salad sandwiches." My face goes red as the bush of wild roses in the backyard, bathed in fire. I walk up close to her where she can feel hot.

"I can still see that bruise," I say and she thwacks me, missing my face, but it punches my neck, and I go blank for a second before I hit the floor. She leaves to check her blown out face in the upstairs mirror. I grab a Pop-Tart un-toasted, steal five sugar cubes and an apple and walk through the tin-covered walkway to the barn. I hate hating my mama. Hate her for taking it off my daddy, the weight of all things crossed and close and pushing down around us. Blue skinks skitter in the ivy and it is a May clear sky today while Confederate jasmine takes control of the air.

Horses' eyes can see a smidgen of movement from straight ahead to almost directly behind, and smell flares their sensitive nostrils. Loki rears up when I open the barn's wide white swing-out doors. The bottoms of the doors look waterlogged and kicked in. I can feel from the door Loki's shake-apart muscles and chisel teeth and strike-out hooves. He is sculpture pretty, sleek and long-legged.

I love this Loki I talk to low. "Settle down, boy," I say. "I brought you some goodies. If you're an easy boy, we'll go for a ride today. Easy boy." His velvety blue mouth lips the sugar cube into his mouth. He swings his long face as he chews, paws at the dirt and pushes his nostril into my pocket, so I pat his flank, sit on the railing and hand him another cube. Soon I have the curb bit in his mouth and bridle over his ears. Mostly the Ratskeller Hunting Club members cannot get this close to Loki without him lashing his hooves out. I slide on bareback and unlatch the gate from his bathroom-tiny stall. It swings out and we lunge into the sunshine two-beat gaited, trotting.

The dew made diamonds on the wild scuppernong vines in the night and sparkle now while red-winged dragonflies buzz off. It's the time of year when cardinals like to chase each other vicious through trees.

Loki shakes under me and I am don't-know-what-might-happen-next scared. He shies at sticks and dead vines and anything snake-twisted. I cling to his mane and use my knees to hang on, thinking how Mama won't let me ride this Loki. She wants me washing the cedar walls of the playroom where kids teach each other cheating card tricks. She wants me starving the roosters so they'll be mad as hens for tonight's fight. She wants me to pluck the bush of wild roses hot for arrangements on the tables which the women only will notice. Sometimes I think she'd just as soon I stiffened over dead. Or maybe she wishes it on her own self.

When I get up to Smitty's place, he is shoeing a red Appaloosa from down the road and the new girl vet is in his colored person barn tending the mule.

"Hello, Miss Dorinda," Smitty says, tipping his Atlanta Braves hat. "I see you got Loki, the hopeless wonder. He ain't throwed you yet?"

"Nope," I say patting Loki's neck.

"He tried to break you Daddy's neck?"

I shake my head no. Un huh, he says, like he owns a peer-in crystal ball and knows more than me. About then, the new girl vet walks out with English riding pants on like in a horse magazine. She is rangey-tall with nutmeg hair and freckles. Her stained-glass blue eyes glimpse into me and I am scared she can crack through so I look away.

"Mule's fine, Smitty," she says, wiping her hands on a smudge-white towel. "I wormed him. He ought to be just fine after a few days of clearing the worms out of his system." A messy job I never did see a girl do, worming a horse. Put tubing up its nose and siphon the milky mix directly to the stomach.

"Met Dorinda, Doctor Emily?" Smitty says. Doctor Emily says no and I say no and I say hey and she says a yankee hello and my heart beats on my ribs as she admires Loki.

"Beautiful—it's a stallion," she says. "You've got a stallion around here? Gorgeous horse," she says. She reaches out to touch Loki's tight neck and he rears up sudden as lightning. Dr. Emily says "Easy boy, easy." She takes out a carrot, flattens her hand like only horse people know how. Loki lip-yanks it away and steps back.

"Dorinda's daddy Mister Henry Carter," Smitty says, like maybe explaining something. "Runs the Hunting Club up the way." Smitty gestures up towards the direction of our house barn waterlogged place.

"Oh. Hmm. With the chickens?" she says. Her stained-glass eyes cut into my dark green ones. I nod and whirl my eyes away from hers. "I don't like what they do with those chickens," she says. My muddy unbreathing insides will not let me speak. It feels like she just said, Oh, you are an ugly, stupid girl through and through, like Daddy says to Mama sometimes when he's Jacked out and picks up an unloaded gun and pushes her in the ribs with it. What does this yankee girl know anyway? It fumes me that she is right.

I pull Loki away and say Bye to Smitty. The girl vet with stained-glass piercing eyes stares a burn into my back all the way through my heart.

"Let me know if you want to breed that horse," Dr. Emily says. "I've got all mares, two Thoroughbreds, a Morgan and an Arabian. But that's a beautiful stallion. I'd be happy for him to stud one of my mares." I walk Loki through the black tar thick of muddy steam road home. My neck throbs where Mama hit me but I do not cry. I no longer do that. It does not help anyway.

I kick and click, use all the tricks to get Loki back into the sloggy barn where the men will pit roosters together tonight to claw to the death. Loki does not want to go back into the sweat-bothered barn. He rears up and almost sends me backwards, but I know how to cling. His neigh has pulled the heavy syrup pull of my mother outside to see me doing razor-sharp exactly what she said don't do. She holds a blue-striped kitchen towel with ice to her struck swelled-up face.

"Get off that horse," she says. "Put him up." I step my eyes from her gaze. Loki rears up again. I cling to his mane. "Dorinda, get off that horse this minute," she says. "You father is off—he's off—"

"I know this means Daddy sits in his engine locked go nowhere car out back listening to the baseball game on the radio. I know Daddy is already Jacked, holding his bottle between his legs with the left hand, right hand up on the seat. I know this means Daddy's feeling like a tornado twister.

I let on like I only see Loki and tell him steady now. He stops and breathes like he's running the big race. The boxwoods, azaleas, ferns, ivy and Virginia Creeper all out-of-control climb around our yard as Mama stands straight as lipstick, waiting. I slide off Loki and say I hate you, murmurous between my teeth.

I walk to cool him down and brush his hair and mane. Then I scoop from the ragged burlap feedsack some corn and oats that he munches and scissors and swallows. I dip a bucket from the outside trough and bring water for him. He sucks it down with the sound of night mosquitoes. Then I get cleaned up to help Mama with doilies and clipped fire roses and half-handful only size tuna salad sandwiches.

This is the summer when no air moves and the sunset bruises the throat of the night. I think this as the women prepare potato salad and green beans and Mama pulls out the half-handful sandwiches from the big Kelvinator in the hose-down kitchen. The men holler from the barn where Loki backs squish-trapped into a corner of his stall, eyes freakish-huge.

"Hush and eat," the women say to kids whose fingers grime the Supreme bread sandwiches and later will slap each other's card hands after dinner. "Hush and eat," my mama says, with her Avon-Ladied "Blushing Beige" covering her secrets.

"Covered it up," I say in front of Mrs. Sutton and Mrs. Hill.

"What's that?" Mrs. Hill says. "Covered what, Lisa Lee?" Mrs. Sutton asks my mama, half-interested. My mama's eyes get scared-shamed, then she looks at me like pure hate. Like I ruined her party. I do not care. "Nothing," she whispers, slitting her eyes at me in warning.

Then I hear clapping of the men like rain and I know that one rooster has zinged the eye out of the other, and Loki nickers loud. Then I hear Daddy shouting.

I run to look in the kids-and-ladies-not-allowed barn. I peek into the waterlogged door and see my daddy Jacked so bad he's weaving. He's gotten on the fence, balanced there and jumps floppy onto Loki's back. Loki rears up like gulf waves in a hurricane and the men roar and hoot. Daddy sits up and grins. Then he bows. Loki's eyes gleam like something drowning.

"Don't! Stop it!" I am screaming. But I'm the only one can hear my voice on the other side of the swing-out barn doors. My voice sounds like from under water. Then Loki rears up and up and up again and throws my daddy on the ground. Daddy's eyes show a flood of fire mad. He staggers up and grabs the bridle off the post as the men all gather around the bathroom-small horse stall.

My daddy starts to backhand blow Loki with the leather reins. He saws Loki's skin with leather, slashes over and over him across Loki's shoulder and chest. He cuts and swings as if to kill as Loki claws at the air with his hooves. "Don't! Stop it!" I scream. Like under water and only I can hear.

But I am wrong. Mama's behind me, breathing so hard, her swell-face, her shouldering this whole thing, this shotgun Daddy's been using for deer hunting. "Dorinda, what—I thought something was wrong—get away from the barn door!"

"They're trying to kill Loki!" I say.

"Don't bother them," she says, panicky. "Your father will be all over me if you bother them, get away from that door and shut up." I stand up from the waterlogged and banged in white barn door; she cradles the gun in her right elbow.

"You bitch," I say and it echoes around the whole green world and comes back at me. "How can you say that? Loki. They're torturing Loki."

She snaps the shotgun and pulls the gun butt up to her heart. When I look at the heart muzzle of the shotgun I see a black hole where I came out of my mama green. I feel myself slip, slip, slip, grabbing the air. I move in the space of no time at all into the busted up light of night that weighs nothing under the trees that snatch at things fallen long time ago out of heaven. I slip and wrestle back up to myself. I can not move to stop and not move to go. I watch for the snap that has already let loose but the gun does not balooey. Just zing, spinning me off her, cut away and I notice the twist of her apron tie flat as a purple umbilical cord, Mama still pointing the gun at me. I wait. So sorrowful.

I hear the men's clinking bottles, smashing and rattling the clattery trash can. Bored after the Daddy throw and Loki beating. My heart is angel wing beating and I've lost. We've lost, she and me. Lost to the quiet haze, the desperate frogs calling mates, lost to the leaves breathing deep ticking of heavy water drops collapsing onto leaves, lost. Cricket stillness edges in and creeps close enough to feel the nothing of a funnel-shaped cloud tornado-like gun muzzle.

"Go ahead and pull the trigger, Mama," I say. "Just go ahead."

The gun catches in her arms and droops, sucks itself out of her hand and clatters to the ground. The surge of every molecule of her blisters the all of me and I grow down. I grow heavy as early morning ocean surf clawing towards ground up grains of sand.

Her eyes downshift and she pales like mother-of-pearl, her wet matted hair clotted in baby finger knots.

I go fleshy and relax, gallop to the gun and pick it up and run. I three-gait it to Loki's trough outside the back of the barn where the women and children and men are not. I pitch the shotgun into the water and it clanks to the bottom.

Mama is at my back, and I feel tomato-frog puffed-up scared red, charged up, and fight-run light. We turn in a circle facing each other like the moon and sun around earth.

"Dorinda. I don't know what came over me. I—"

"Shut up," I say. And me, I shut up. "Shut up." And I stamp past her out into the big open throat of the woods so my muddy insides can dry.

The storm of every night downpour ends the party. The winds rip and thunder, lightning smacks and people climb in their cars, slam the doors, spit their engines on and glow their headlights out towards town.

I sit under the biggest live oak alive. Alive. Alive and sweat-soaked in this electric storm. Limbs get torn from trees and the world dampens. The rain finally crackles and pounds the ground. Alive and wet, hidden under the cloak of night.

In the people screaming silence afterwards I am hush-and-eat quiet, waiting for Mama and Daddy to sleep. Then I rise up wet and coated with protective sticky of skin changing and whish the church barn door open. Loki's coat stickies with blood on his chest and he stamps and quivers his withers and I do not sob but slosh in the powder fog of after rain with Loki on a rope behind me.

I slog up through the woods in the fumes of cricket choirs to Smitty's. I crest the hill and Smitty's lights have closed in the wet. Back down the other side of the hill I see bonfire light at Dr. Emily's house. I clop-clop up to Dr. Emily's egg-blue house on the hill forbidden and clean.

Mosquitoes buzz around and I bang on the door of the slim house. I knock loud. Knock again. The door does not open but I hear voices in the barn behind and I clop with Loki back there. Dr. Emily and Smitty are blinking in the light of her yellow lantern as she is squatted over her cow in the stall in labor.

"Hello, Dorinda," Dr. Emily says from the ground, like I've come to take tea. Vets take calls in the black night with sticky girls and bloody horses so she does not slam up on me. "What's going on?"

"Loki," I say pushing back the smash and roar. "Loki needs to get away—" My voice moon-jumps and wavers like heat on the tar road.

"Oh, my god, who—" Dr. Emily says standing up.

"That party going on down the road," Smitty says. He hooks the lamp on the barn wall stick-out wood. "I can handle the cow, Doctor Emily, if you want to check the horse over."

"What—" she says.

"My daddy." I hold my breath.

"What on earth?"

"Best not be asking too many questions, Doctor Emily," Smitty says. "Henry Carter runs the club over the hill."

"Please get my horse safe," I say. "He's too big and frisky for that barn dark."

"I see." She takes the reins from me.

"Far away, where he can't find Loki," I say.

She hesitates, studying Loki's bloody cuts. "Not too deep, but my god, he did this with—"

"I wouldn't be asking too many questions," Smitty says.

"I know a place where he can have pastures. Open barn," she says, patting his forehead. Loki's tired closes over his skittishness with Dr. Emily.

"He's had a bad night," I say. I hug him good-bye smelling sour and grassy and pissy, sticky and wet and heat unlocked onto me. Then I back step away from my black horse, black as the ivory-inlaid table Daddy got from the Korea war.

I walk away, heading back to the waterlogged barn and tiny house. Somewhere. "Dorinda?" Dr. Emily says, even though her cow is starting to bellow the calf out of her now. "You can come up here anytime, you know. Ride the mares." My angel heart opens and I am slipping again under the weight of trees and things of women and I want to race away. I want to race into her arms and say Please, let me come live with you where things seem like they keep moving. No stuck fog breathing gun muzzles and no Jack. Where things are so blue quiet as your stained-glass eyes. I lower my dark green eyes and close up my angel to protect me in the dark.

"I don't know. Maybe," I say shrugging a shoulder. I turn again and keep walking away somewhere. Past me where I can see pasture and a light small barn dry, somewhere past the black swells that rise up and rise up and rise up, the black swell of it all as the cow grunts and I hear Dr. Emily's Oh! Get it on its legs! in pajama-blue joy with the calf born. And for what seems like the first time, I come up. One step. Another step. I come up. Another step on the black tar road shiny in the rain-soaked night, I come up for air.

SHEER CURTAINS GOING DOWN

First time I laid eyes on Cookie Johnson, she tiptoed down the clay road, yellow and white polka dot ribbons in her black pigtails, and I ached to talk to her. The late summer trees had deep greened, good enough to eat. I Tennessee-Walkered my old horse Stella up beside her. Cookie barefooted her brown feet across the road rocks, sharp.

I figured her my age, eleven. She wore a ribbon-matching shorts outfit of yellow, only faded. Somebody'd bought her those bright ribbons. I'd seen them in the Gibbs French Shoppe downtown.

I'd seen Cookie downtown in the McCroy's Department store with a fountain Coke stand, a sip-and-look bar where across the street stood the Florida State Capitol. Also a snack bar where a "coloreds only" bathroom had stood outside just a few years before. I'd spied her once, me deciding between Beatles records "Eight Days a Week" and "Can't Buy me Love." She had stood over the Motown LP's charting with her eyes Diana Ross and the Supremes and the Four Tops records.

Now she turned and looked up at me, and I gave her my 'I'm sorry' look cause I owned a horse. She gave me a hard, deep-in-the-eyes black girl look that said 'I don't give a damn.'

One of two black girls in the fifth grade at Kate Sullivan Elementary last year, Cookie always stood out for me.

"Hey," I said.

"Hey." She looked away, tiptoeing across the gravel, arms stretched out beside her for balance. I kicked Stella to catch up to her.

"I like your ribbons," I said. "You get them at Gibbs?"

"Uh-huh," she said, not looking at me but at the jump and sharp of rocks on bare feet.

"What are you doing down here?" I said.

"Living," she said.

"You want to ride my horse?" I said. She halted and looked up with shaded eyes, like a filmy white curtain in a window that came down.

"Girl, you asking for trouble," she said.

"Huh-uh," I said. I slid off saddlefree Stella, and stood next to this girl, and looked up. She already pushed up towards six feet tall. Near a foot ahead of me. "You scared or something?" I said.

"No, I ain't scared," she said, glancing up the white folks road, then down the colored people road.

"Let's go down in here," I said, pointing to the rut road through Mr. Pipps' woods. The trees, underbrush and overgrown grass could swallow us up. If my Mama saw me, she'd put me on restrictions. "No riding horses for a week if you're gonna ride nigras on them," I could hear her say.

I know what Daddy would have said. He'd have said he'd skin me alive.

"You don't live around here," I said, looking over at Cookie. She eyed Stella like she didn't trust her. People who hung around people and not horses acted like that, staring up around at the horse's tall back like they couldn't believe horse hugeness, their eyes asking would this horse bite or kick. "Stella's her name. See the white star between her eyes? Don't worry, she's old. She won't do anything." I patted Stella's plump flank. "What you doing here?"

"I'm living with my Aunt Jesse this summer, nosy girl," she said, reaching out her palm and touching Stella's neck.

"Jesse's your aunt?" I said.

"Uh huh," she said, running her hand down Stella's sleek neck, then smearing the loose sweaty hairs on her bare leg. We crossed over the ditch and moved onto the right hand rut. Jesse was the closest black lady living on the hill. Only our paved lane and the woods between separated us from her. The old Mr. Pipps had deeded Jesse's daddy three acres when he'd freed him from slavery. Jesse owned the land now. A man never laid up at Jesse's, but kids always came and went from her two-bedroom house and three acres. The few kids from up the hill walked, biked or rode down to visit her and to watch the 80-year-old Jesse and her big black pot boiling laundry. She let us pick plums and peaches in her yard, and sold us nickel sugar cane in summertime. Our parents said she knew her place, so they didn't mind our visits.

I laced my fingers together and stooped to offer a hand-stirrup for Cookie to boost up onto Stella.

"Put your left foot in here and step up, then throw your right leg around," I said. She looked at me with a smoldering pause. "Come on, I won't drop you." She hitched up easy, but grabbed Stella's mane tight. I led Stella by the reins down into the wild grasses and oak trees to shade us overhead. I told her I, Rayann Wood, hated school, loved horses. She, Cookie Johnson, hated school and loved the picture show.

I told her how my teacher Mrs. Searcy had found out we formed the I-hate-Mrs.-Searcy club. "She a mean old hog," Cookie said. She'd had Mrs. McCloud who everybody wanted for a teacher, with pretty skin and smelling like powder. When you walked to her desk, she put her arm around you like she meant it. She yelled hardly ever. But Mrs. McCloud couldn't make things okay for Cookie at school. Cookie'd always played alone or with the only other black girl on the playground.

Some kids had held their noses when they played Capture the Flag on her team, she told me.

We passed August blackberries, picking and eating. They burst big, juicy and sweet in our mouths, our lips a purple stain after. The more we walked, the looser Cookie's grip got on Stella's mane. We followed the path to the back side of Pipps' pond, and Stella automatically stopped and stooped to drink. I hand stirruped another offer to get her down. The sheer curtain dropped over her eyes again. She shook her head and said, "Move out the way," and she slid off like I had, swinging her right leg over and sliding her butt down, landing feet first on the ground. Stella stepped into the pond and slurped water. Cookie laughed aloud at Stella's slurp.

We ankle-waded and I said my favorite singing group was The Beach Boys. Cookie rolled her eyes and said only, Gladys Knight.

"You hungry?" I said, pulling out the brown paper bag I'd stashed in the backside of my shorts waistband.

"A little," she said. "What you got in that bag?" I pulled out a peanut butter and jelly sandwich, wax paper wrapped. The bread had mushed up and the jelly'd bled through.

"I ain't eating none of that," Cookie said.

"Me neither," I said. I palmed the browned banana. "Ooo, yuk, this either," I said.

"Maybe your horse want it," Cookie said. I flattened out my hand, sandwich in it. Stella sniffed, furry mouth tickling my fingers. She yanked the sandwich between her teeth and lipped it into her mouth.

"She's eating it!" I said. We screamed a star-blooming laugh. Stella reared her head back, munched on that sandwich, big eyes startley. We laughed fall-down hard together on the grass beside the splishy pond. We held our stomachs. The sky shouted blue and Stella munched away nodding her head. I turned my head over laughing and looked at this girl, Cookie Johnson, and she looked at me. She was a black girl. She got quiet and stared back at me, the film coming over her eyes, the wrinkles of her laughing face-skin evaporating. She remembered, too. I was white. The breeze rustled and snapped the trees overhead.

"Your old horse crazy," she said. We both broke out laughing again.

She leaped back onto Stella and I led them out to the road. When we reached Pipps' road, I looked both ways—up the hill and down—and I turned to Cookie.

"You want to see my secret hideout?" I noticed that sheer curtain fall across Cookie's eyes yet again.

"What for?" she said.

"We can build us a house," I said. She shrugged, darting eyes away from mine. "I'll make Rice Krispies marshmallow treats," I said.

"Tomorrow," she said.

"Same time?" I said. She nodded. I walked her on Stella up Jesse's rut road to her two-bedroom white house on three acres. Jesse rocked in her beat up chair on the porch, smoking a cigar. When she eyed us, she stopped, hand and cigar froze in midair.

"What you girls doing?" she said, sitting up straight and still as a clock not running.

"I'm riding this tired horse, Aunt Jesse. It won't do nothing bad, he old," Cookie said.

"She," I said. "Stella. She's a she."

"Rayann, you best get on home, you hear?" Jesse stood, left hand on her back, and limped to the door. "Cookie Johnson, get your sassy self in this house and I don't mean later." She used the cigar with her right hand to point out her meaning.

"Yes, ma'am," Cookie said.

"Tomorrow," I whispered. She didn't answer.

I waited a long tree-shade time, holding a tin foil full of Rice Krispies treats. I'd sneaked them out easy. Mama was sewing a new linen tablecloth with napkins to match. Hand projects helped her. The more my daddy drank, the more hand projects she found, and the less attention she could pay to other things.

Daddy worked back-breaker hours at the hospital and baby doctor-
ing kept him from home. But he dozed with the TV flickering and
Scotch-on-the-rocks on the table beside in the den. Some nights he didn't
show up, even when not on call. He'd show up the next morning, hair
mussed up and looking sheepish and barnslept. If Mama told him I'd
been bad, he'd give me licks, hard with a skinny leather belt.

He joked about a black welfare patient, named Fraji Lee. He'd asked
Fraji Lee's mama where she found that name, and she said off the side
of a box, Fraji Lee, handle with care. I laughed at that one. I wondered
if Cookie would.

Finally I heard rustling to the left, Jesse's side of the woods. Cookie
appeared with two corn husks.

"Girl, you call this a hideout?" she said, glancing around. I shrugged.
"Well, you need something on the ground, keep the poison ivy off your
legs." She spotted the Rice Krispies treats.

"Want one?" I said, stretching out to offer the treats. She chose two
and ate. "What's that corn for?" I asked.

"Smoking," she said, mouth full. I must have looked uneasy. "Smoking corn silks. My cousin told me he smokes them. Want to try?"

My heart fast-thumped. "Yeah!" I said. This would be the best
August ever, the best hideout in town, maybe even in the country, maybe
in the world, I thought as Cookie pulled off corn silks and rolled two in
corn shucks. She handed me a rolled cigarette. She struck a kitchen-
snitched match and held the flame up for me.

"Well?" she said. "You chicken?" I shook my head no and let her
light it. She told me to breathe in. I did and then started coughing till I
thought I'd blow up blue in the face. She laughed loud enough to hear
a mile off. Then she lit her own and coughed herself.

"See?" I said. She said it didn't bother her, made her high and she
smoked about five cough-puffs off hers.

"It's our peace pipe," I said. "We're sworn to secrecy. We can't
ever tell about this place. Promise?" Cookie nodded a cough and

smashed out her cornsilk cigarette. We munched on treats while I asked her the scariest thing she ever saw. She said she didn't know, what kinda dumb question was that?

I told her about Terry McHugh who'd gotten in second grade leukemia and how he'd disappeared from school. Then one day the teacher marched the class outside to say hey to Terry who'd come up to visit. Our principal instructed him to stand across the street and wave, even though the teachers had explained to us that leukemia wasn't contagious.

"His face was all swole up and he'd got so fat," I said crunching on Krispies and marshmallow. "He was always skinny and all of the sudden, boom, like a water balloon. And white as a sheet. He died two weeks later."

"All white people's white as a sheet," Cookie said, and picked up another Rice Krispies Treat. "Well, I got a uncle who's part white and he's got one green eye and one brown. The brown one don't work, neither. Got a filmy white over it and it wander around in his head. The green one will be looking right at you and the brown one just go in circles and over to one side, then the other." I said yuk and she seemed content with gross-outing me.

We finished off the treats and gathered leaves to use as our floor and spread them around. After a couple of hours, I heard Mama calling me.

"I gotta go," I said. "When do you want to meet again?"

Cookie shrugged and looked at the ground. "Maybe we shouldn't," she said. "Aunt Jesse told me I shouldn't have rode on your horse."

"Come on," I said. "I'll bring chocolate chip cookies next time."

She said, "All right, then, how about Sunday after church?"

Cookie and I met all month, and found vines for our hideout to disguise it. We snitched an old horse blanket and packed down a floor with it. We dirty joked and I asked her if she knew a girl caught pregnancy from French kissing. She said, "You crazy, girl," and gave me how-it-really-worked details.

"I'll never do that," I said, "It's too crazy."

"Shoot," she said. "You don't know what you'll do." I told her I bet my parents never did that and she said, "Sure they did."

We got to where we smoked cornsilk cigarettes with no cough and sometimes we imitated songs we liked and we'd get to laughing hard, forgetting to be taped-up quiet and secret. My mama asked me where was I disappearing to those afternoons and I said, "Just taking walks in the woods." She looked at me like I better be telling the truth.

One day when we met, a bright idea danced upon me.

"Tomorrow night's the first college football game, not really a football game, but the team playing against itself," I said.

"I can't go with you to no football game," she said. Black people didn't go to the white college football games. They had their own college football games on their town's side.

"No. I mean, Mama and Daddy are going out and we got a baby-sitter. But she's not so smart, an old lady, and I can sneak out. Can you sneak out and meet me?"

"No. No, ma'am, I can't. We could get into big trouble, Miss Smarty Pants Rayann. No; I'm telling you no." But I said we'd go out after ten, when Jesse was hummed off to sleep. I'd pretend to turn out my light, crawl into bed and then instead sneak out Mama and Daddy's sliding glass door.

"It'll be easy," I said. "Come on. What? You chicken?"

She said, "I'm no chicken, never, just a body has to be careful."

"Well, it'll be the last time we get to see each other in—maybe forever and ever. Next week school starts, you know," I said.

"Okay, Rayann," she said with a sigh like a fire field burning out to black earth.

"Ten o'clock," I said. "And I'll make this sound to show it's me. Hooo hooo hooo." My favorite sound of late afternoon. The sound of the mourning dove, and it only sounded in that purplish-blue time between day and night.

The next night the six o'clock news reported three guys had escaped from the Federal Correctional Institute down the Truck Route about a mile. The newsman said to watch out for them, they might head for town to get food and water. Since we lived out in the country, I figured the escaped F.C.I. guys wouldn't come our way. Mama told the baby-sitter to keep the doors locked, and to make sure I didn't take a step outside even to check on the dogs.

At nine-thirty I pretended to yawn and stretch and tell the baby-sitter how worn out I felt. I'll go to bed now, I said, and turned into my room, clicked off the light and got into bed with my clothes on. As the clock tick-tocked, I felt under the sheets where I'd sneaked the flashlight. I plucked it on and off. I stuffed the red pears I'd stolen from the kitchen into my tucked in shirt. At five till ten, I tiptoed to the door. I could hear the TV blaring as I slipped across the lit hallway, and dove quietly into Mama and Daddy's room.

"Rayann, is that you?" the baby-sitter called from the family room. She'd turned the TV down.

"Yes, ma'am, I'm just going to the bathroom," I said.

"In your parents' room?"

My palms sweated smeary. "I like this bathroom better," I said, poking my head into the hall. The toilet paper's softer." She shook her head and turned back to the TV.

I flushed the toilet, then walked back to my room. I figured I better wait and hope she'd drop asleep. Then I started thinking. I could slip the screens out my window and jump down from the ledge, a ten foot drop.

I shut my bedroom door, unlatched the screen, pushed it out the front, climbed up my bookcase, slung my legs over and lowered the window back. I'd have to pull up the ladder to climb back in. I hung from the ledge, feeling the pears squash into my stomach, then I let go.

I hit the ground and fell on my butt, but I got up and started walking across the front yard where a three-quarter moon shone down. The moon speckled the pathway to the fort as I crossed the oak-covered lane and ducked into the woods. I turned on the flashlight, and could hear Cookie. "Hooo hooo hooo," she said, soft as summer breeze on my face.

"Here I am," I whispered.

"Well, get your ass in here," she said. "It ain't safe making sounds at night that sposed to happen in the afternoon." She sounded scared. I ducked into our viney hideout and shone the flashlight on her. Her eyes looked clear brown in the night. "Was Jesse asleep?" I asked.

"Yeah. I jumped from the bedroom window. Put out that light, you want to get caught?" she said, blinking.

"I had to go out my window, too," I said. When I clicked off the flashlight, the moon beamed on our hideout. I told her the toilet paper excuse, and we laughed. We shared a cornsilk cigarette and a pear, and I told her my mama said never to eat after a colored person.

"Seems like the richer folks gets, the more scared they gets."

"About what?"

"About other peoples. What people's gonna take from them good," she said, "or give them that's bad." A dog barked nearby.

We shared a second pear. Something rustled in the leaves, stepping or creeping through the woods. We looked at each other in the moonlight, petrified. We huddled together and could hear each other's breaths.

"Did you know three convicts got out of F.C.I.?" I whispered.

"No," she said and snuggled closer to me. Twigs snapped around us. "We gonna die, ain't we?"

"I don't know," I said and flung my arms around her. She pulled hers around me. The crickets snickity-snickitied. The leaf-rustling, twig-snapping kept up, around the side of the hideout. Then it headed off out towards the lane.

Cookie whispered a story about the colored lady raped by white convicts about three years ago down on Miccosukee Road.

"Then they cut her open with a knife." She paused. "From her slit up to her throat," she whispered. We laid down in the cool night air, the whir of crickets all around us, our arms around each other. I whispered to her about three black men from out-of-state who visited the BlueBird Cafe in Frenchtown, the colored part of town.

"They went upstairs to the whorehouse and paid for a white woman," I whispered, "then they tied her naked to a chair and cut off her boobs. Then scalped her." I could hear the dog barking nearby. "They say the blood leaked through the wood floor on people eating peas and rice and drinking beer downstairs."

We both started crying, and saying we would miss our mama and daddy even if they weren't perfect, and we confided in each other our one wish we'd have if God came down now and granted it to us before we died. I wished for a black stallion colt I could train myself. She wished she could be a movie star. People would send her flowers every day, she said.

We whimpered until we must have fallen asleep. We both woke up hearing Jesse call out, "Cookie?" and Daddy yell, "Rayann!"

"I think they over here someplace, Mr. Wood," we heard Jesse say. "Seems like this the way Cookie been headed when she disappear sometimes." Next thing we knew, Jesse's stooped self stood with a lantern peering in.

"Rayann Wood, what in God's name do you think you're doing?" Daddy said, behind her. I didn't say a thing. I dreaded what might happen when I got home. Once Daddy'd whipped me with a belt for sassing him back, so I never sassed him again. He'd been drinking, the way he slurred it. I scrambled up and stood in front of him. Cookie crawled out behind me.

"And look at you, girl," Jesse said to Cookie. "Ain't you shamed? Shamed!"

"Jesse," Daddy said, "what do you know about this? What's going on here?"

"I don't know, Mr. Wood," Jesse said. She sounded scared herself. "I seen Miss Rayann riding Cookie on her big old horse one time. I told Rayann to get herself home. Cookie, she been running off over here—"

"Well, keep your pickaninnies on your own property," he said. For a minute only the shaking of the dogwood leaves sounded in the wind overhead. Dogwoods were the first to change colors in the fall. I didn't know whether to be more ashamed of me or embarrassed of Daddy. An ache spilled into my arms and legs and chest. "Is it understood?" Daddy said.

"Yessir," Jesse said. Then it grew hysterical quiet, like something wild you come across in the woods dead before the flies come. I could barely stand to look at Cookie, but I did. I made her out in the moonlight. That film like white curtains came over her eyes before she looked to the ground and stuck her eyes there, then turned away, her aunt pinching on her arm hard.

"Come on, Rayann, what the hell's got into you?" Daddy said, jerking me by the arm. I didn't know; I didn't say. He stopped and smacked me across the face. "You know how I feel about this sort of thing," he said. Alcohol coated his breath. My stomach felt punched. I knew not to say anything, but to follow him on home.

He lectured me through the woods about how I could get strange diseases from hanging around the coloreds. I didn't talk, but I was sure what I heard. As the creamy moonlight hit my skin when we crossed the lane, it spun through me like music. It was the Hooo hooo hooo of the mourning dove.

SWALLOWS DANCE

I'm inspecting the damage at my place, is why I'm out here and not downriver at Fowler's Bluff where I've stayed for months now. All the chicken-coop cages William helped me build are twisted and torn out where I used to keep pelicans who gulped down fishhooks or egrets with broken wings. This saddens me, and I think of what's lost and how William showed me that winter he stayed with me how to patch together long orange electric cords to a socket, screwing in a hundred watt bulb to keep the birds and animals warm, while ducks and geese from north stopped off for seed, then headed south to the gulf and on.

My Creek grandma, dead now, told me this place means Where Wind Slices a Swallow Dancing. That's pretty close, I think. Here at the riverbend a few miles before the Suwannee River meets the gulf, wind fire-spins its way across the flat saltwater surface and hot-thrashes through saw grass to the brackish water, up the river, tearing the guts open of cypress trees. It hurls its way through lean pines, ripping live oak limbs that later squawk in the breeze, like to remind me of what happened to William, a college teacher in biology tired of college teaching in biology, just wanting to live it, he'd said.

Even the foxes who lost their mama are gone. And that damn black cat with a bobcat tail. She came sniffing and creeping on tiptoe looking for William and didn't find him so stuck that tail upwards to heaven walking right past me back to Fowler's Bluff.

Of the three buildings, the house me and William lived in holds itself up out of the flooded yard most. Except where the cypress tree tops sit smack where the glass of the bedroom window used to be. The old Airstream painted redwood by William to match my house and Grandma's old shotgun shack looks worse. The Airstream flipped like a gopher turtle on its back, and Grandma's floor has sagged till it's fallen out. Nobody's lived in that house since she died six years ago.

The last of the floodwater sun-spangles across the yard, covering the dollar weed, the ragweed and other plants Grandma said made Indian medicine. At the gate, morning glory vines start to green out again, and the yellow No Trespassing sign has faded. And no cat, Ibo, as William called her, saying Ibo meant black in African, the Ibo tribe proud of their color. William never liked Sambo, the name they gave our big black cat with a bobcat tail down at Fowler's Bluff.

That's where Ibo got snatched up by me when those hunters from out of state with semi-automatics camped out. She took up with them from before being wild, them throwing her scraps of chicken and fishbait, but the hunting dogs dogged her and would every now and again run her off. One evening a bird-dog picked that black cat up by the neck and shook and shook till I came off Zach Creech's dock on Fowler's Bluff, my hand bleeding from tearing a palmetto branch by the saw-toothed stem. I must have been a sight waving that big branch and screaming till that dog dropped Ibo out of his mouth and cowered away.

I took that damn black cat back to my place to check if her neck got broke. It had not. But that cat, after I squeezed some cold water on her neck sticky with blood, came to. She up and lunged at my arm, tearing up the skin and bit deep before she tore off out the front door. Never forgave me, wouldn't let me touch her. And still I fed her and still she ate from the bowl and drank milk, too.

Which puzzled me, how William had settled down that cat and kept her away from the wild hurt bird cages. Kept that cat rubbing up by his side. It was a way William had on kids, animals and grown-ups, even those hunters with semi-automatics. His throw-down size did not hurt, either. Not a handsome man, but thick as a boat bow, tall as any man around here. Fingers near thick as my wrists. I only came up around the bottom of William's ribcage. He loved to read books. That did not keep him from thoughtfulness. He'd drop a book on his stomach open and look out at the river with the cicadas going, thinking.

"Muzeta," he'd say, "Lu Creech just got that baby of hers out of the hospital. I think we ought to take them some dinner and see if they need some baby supplies." He drove women in town wild from that kind of thinking, talking, laughing easy and quick like a woman. Viv and Miriam Swaim at the bar one Thursday, my night to town, talked about his homeliness and asked me once who got on top when we did it. I asked them if they both wanted a fist in the belly or a toss into the gulf. I saw the Swaim sisters while we sat talking fish, eyeballing William's arms when he'd hoist a split-open and gutted shark up the chain of the weighing scale at the fish house where I worked three days a week.

The fish house and Cedars Bar is what I call town, where the semi rigs came to pick up fresh turtle, stone crab claws, redfish and shrimp to pack up and send to places you read about in the paper like California and New York. Town, where after a fishing day, men and women came to drink at the confluence of the gulf and the river, where if you got a phone call, and you were not around, everybody—the Swaims, Dori and Orrie Hamm the crabbers, Snook the shrimper—they'd all talk to that person on the phone anyway.

This place I called town, where before William came I could pull up in Grandma's old gray oyster boat with the orange-painted bottom in a night when I swear the stars blued in a dark green sky. The jukebox would be wailing and boom-booming and the red and white beer light shone in the window. There I'd be finding out what days the next week I'd need to come weigh fish, collecting hurt animals along the way that people'd stashed up, them knowing what work I did up where Wind Slices a Swallow Dancing with nursing these animals back to health.

The Swaim sisters and Hamm brothers said William put a hex on me, "a way," a stay-at-home way and a wear-dresses way. That's pretty close, I think, since I wore just old shorts and a ripped out t-shirt and went barefoot most times before William. Grit under the toenails and smelling like a wild injured animal ever since Daddy rammed me up against the wall of the trailer on Goose Cove when I was sixteen and did his thing like a big wind to me. That's as long as I've been out of school and living at Grandma's place away from most things, like men. Cut off and reviving injured birds and hoisting gutted fish so I could buy some refrigerator food for myself. Fishing for river bass with a spear, Grandma's medicine bag leather-strapped around my neck to keep no-see-ums and mosquitoes from biting.

That's how I met William, while I was rounding the corner of the riverbank with a cormorant who'd got tangled in fishing line inside a paper sack I held, that blackbird rattling around in the bag. William chestdeep in the river with plastic bags and a mask, doing his study for the college in the city where cars growled and thrashed around each other fast as Where Wind Slices a Swallow Dancing. The city, where I never go. His project to study some tiny water animals you can not see with your eyes, to check on how much gas and oil had slid off the highway bridges, poisoning up the water.

And him being taken with this half-naked and injured-bird-smelling blackhaired woman with a medicine bag and a paper bag I do not try to understand, except he'd studied Indians and figured me for one. I flushed at the carved out shape of his shoulders and arms as he pulled up the mask and smiled the smile that breezed over me, that breeze I had not felt in eight years since high school in the back of a truck with a boy wearing a wide straw hat from Bronson, whose daddy owned cattle. That breeze that would turn to wind on William.

Painting the houses and the trailer, fixing up new cages for the injured birds and getting Grandma's station wagon running was what other hex and way William put on me. And how on Sundays he'd make a dry wood fire, I'd cut palmettos, carving away the fan and splitting the stem, sharpening the forks. We'd set bacon over the fire, or sausage or sweet potatoes or soda biscuits and have a big Sunday meal.

He brought his boom box and we'd listen to Otis Redding or James Taylor and share a quart of beer. We danced in the living room instead of town so I quit getting fighting-drunk on Thursday nights. We even cleaned out the back porch from old chicken coop wire, ruined lawn mowers, and stretched a two-person hammock and strung a light up to read by at night. William brought his VCR and movies in languages I did not understand but that made me cry and laugh and he would let me hang in his carved out muscle arms. William was hexing my life more than a stay-at-home or wearing-dresses way can show.

In the summer we trolled in Grandma's oyster boat down to Fowler's Bluff where William loved to go. Schools of fish would flutter by in the clear water and I'd kiss him hard at the island in the middle of the river called Kiss-Me-Quick. Then down to Fowler's Bluff where they say an old Spanish treasure is buried but nobody can find it. I'd sing songs about it, and William listened and even hummed along sometimes.

I crooned the song Grandma had taught me about how this huge hurricane came through a hundred years ago and brought with it a tidal wave over fifty feet high, even up here to the Suwannee River, and washed out the whole town. That being the reason town is no town really. And some Spanish pirates who stole treasure then came back to look for it after the wind sliced its swallowing dance, and they could not remember what two cypress trees they buried it under in the water and they fought until they killed each other right under the two cypress trees at Fowler's Bluff.

Every now and again some rich real estate man from the city comes down with a bulldozer, sure he's found the treasure spot, but what they dig up out of the hole is old Indian pipes, pieces of clay pottery and arrowheads. William had rolled me on top of him in the boat and said, "Those are treasures," meaning I don't know if my breasts he grabbed or the pottery and whatall.

During winter, I'd go find lighter pine wood and cypress and cedar to smell up the house good in the wood stove and cover the tops and part of the sides of cages with clear plastic to keep the animals warm. Most stayed alive winters and got to wailing when the up-north geese Vee'd their way across the river.

Late that winter, Ibo birthed four baby kittens, all bobtailed, two with bobcat-gray brown stripes, spots and high backs, so I knew she'd been prowling in the scrub. She purred those kittens out, pushing them onto the sofa in the living room.

So sitting down to watch a TV news show or even to dance to Otis Redding meant dealing with Ibo hurling up her back in a great lightning-backed black terror and her hissing out that slicing wind talk. At me anyway, her not ever forgetting about the ice cold water I poured on her neck. But not William. Ibo allowed William to put a bear fat finger on each kitten and she'd purr proud. Me, I'd walk into the room and up went her back. Once I turned on the TV and she lurched at my back, and I stood up a hollering wind and William raced through the front door to find that cat stuck on my back and me cussing the cat, snatching my arms around, turning, trying to get her off me, and her clutching for dear life. William roared a laugh at that sight and pretended to make me get myself out of this mess alone. Then he walked his bear walk up to us and put a giant hand on both our backs and talked Ibo up into his arms.

Soon spring came and the bobcat pups swarmed the house and when I threw them out they tried to squeeze through the chicken fences and get to the injured birds, which started up a fuss. William coaxed them into a chair in the bedroom and out of irritating the birds with his hex on things.

And that was the spring it all happened, that I am trying to tell about, the spring of Ibo and her bobcat pups, and what I can remember of the rest. And this, the afternoon of heavy thunderheads hissing and slicing a wind around, me and William on the back porch. The back kitchen door with a big glass window shut. Us in the hammock purring at each other and laughing like people do when they're flirting, then me glancing out the screen to see a tall pine bend almost clear to the ground and hearing the moan of it. The wrong kind of moan, and for some reason I got off him and stood up and William sat his large self up in the hammock and the sidestep of the wind that slices a swallowing dance swung its way through the whole yard. It happened fast but it goes through my mind slow, too, now, how I screamed and said Look out! and I ducked down into my own lap on the floor, hands covering up my head, and the pine tree out the front snapped and tumped over pushing its topneedled crown through the roof, falling right at the back door. Sending a plate-sized triangle of glass as William stood up, shooting it right into his gut.

Then it got quiet, the wind taking another breath as William gasped for his and pulled out the glass with a slide of blood on it gone some four or five inches deep and a spread hand across. He held that bloody slice of glass and looked at it, then at me, and then at his gut open and he pushed it closed and got white-faced as the blood from his pushing himself shut splatted on the wood floor. He laid the triangle of glass down on the hammock like it was priceless as a baby as he held his gut with his right hand.

"Town," I said, since we had no phone, and I ran to get an armful of towels. We got into Grandma's gray oyster boat, William sitting on the bottom, our hair and skin soaked as the towels turned pink around his middle and him not talking. In town they could call the city and send a helicopter out.

The way the wind blew, it turned Grandma's boat into a turtle swirl and the moon would not show its head in the scarred-up sky; the towels started to red. William only breathed and spittled rain from his lips and clunked his head on the hard boat seat. I turned the five-horse motor off and started to row to keep us from flowing backwards and him trying not to groan or to slide around, thinking that I rowed a way towards town, but we had not even made Fowler's Bluff yet. I grew a dark note in my gut and throat, in my sleep-wanting eyes, and that's when I knew it, it falling on me like waking up from a hot nap. And I knew it all since I'd passed the third moon with no blood passing.

"I'm pumping," I said. "William?" He raised his face to me in a fleshy question. "I'm pumping up a baby in here." I pointed to my gut and light spread over the wild air and his head snapped back down at the seat of the boat. He smiled then, I saw a spiky smile scratch over his face. And the wind drove into the boat and to keep me company I sang to him when we got to Fowler's Bluff about the treasure lost, about the real estate men coming in and digging, not finding gold but pottery and pipes. I sang about how Ibo had lunged at my back and how I danced in circles trying to get her off. I chanted these stories in the rain and wind that pushed the boat sideways into a big oak limb and punched a hole in the boat. The bottom of the boat turned black-red and I pulled up to the bank where the two cypress trees stood, using the oars for sides and old fish net for bottom and made a moving bed to carry William in over the marshes and saw grasses and dunes to town. All night I pulled that two-hundred pound bed over white-peppered sand and puddles, through spider webs and brush, veering around fallen-down trees and stopping for swallowing winds till they passed. And then I got to the other side of Goose Cove where I could hear the waves of the gulf growling and throwing fast curls up at the shore. But the daybreak rang in a different light to town, and I noticed the towels around William's middle had a brown-red tint to them, soaked through and dripping from the nylon net bottoms. The tops of the oars looked red-painted in smears from my hand-blisters bleeding after rowing and pulling, and that still-stuck smile sat on William's face resting on the oyster nets, wrapped in towels and still.

I numbed when I got the moving bed to the bar and Zach ran out with a big army blanket, looked down at the bed and said, "Holy Christ." He covered up William, even his face. Viv and Miriam came down and I think the helicopter landed a block over in the clearing. When Viv and Miriam brought white sheets and took the blanket off William and started taking off the towels, that's when I lunged at Viv or maybe it was Miriam. And Zach, he pulled me off which is just at the same time my knees went under and I lost sight of all things but shut down black.

The helicopter whirred me to the hospital where I woke up two days later to Lu holding my hand in the hospital bed and telling me the baby was holding fine inside me and I needed to stay up at Fowler's Bluff till the flood went down and I strengthened, and I said I had to get back to the sick birds.

"They're all gone, Muzeta," she said. "The wind sliced open the cages."

So Fowler's Bluff where the treasure's still buried is where I've been staying these summer months, not talking but drinking a milk quart a day at the Creeches and repairing the gray oyster boat. At the fish house the boys won't let me lift, so I clean fish instead, slicing a knife down their middles, opening them and scraping out the guts, flopping them on the scale and jotting down the weight, not talking and everybody glancing at my shut mouth and getting-big belly.

I see William's cat, that damn Ibo and her four cubs crouching about, getting a saucer of milk from the Creeches, her feeling lonely and hungry, scratching on the screen. I feel I will bust with this stomach-stretching baby in me but lately I want that damn Ibo back. I want to go home to Grandma's and set up house for the coming girl baby. Up at the doctor's office they can put a seeing tool on my stomach and view the baby on the TV screen. Big bones and head, especially fingers. I see in town more men with semi-automatics; the Swaims and Creeches and Snooks growing creases around their eyes and balding heads and sagging necks and breasts. The thought of beer turns my stomach, but I got cages for injured birds to fix and a big bear-size hole up between the treasure ship hole and home to tend, and I feel I may just be waking up.

So I'll grab that Ibo by the neck and her cubs, too, and put them in a sack and take them scratching and clawing in the back all the way out to where the wind can sometimes slice and swallow, back to my red home, and fix up the other bedroom for the bear-sized baby girl to come.

BRING BUFFALO PUNCH

I spy my mama fetched fashionable in cat sun glasses, a mod shift, sculpted blonde beehive and belly smooth skin. But I watch her tear the edges of her paper napkin into dusting fringes on her lap. The whole family has come over to Grandma Fleeta's farmhouse for Mama's birthday. Everybody means Daddy, Grandma, aunts and uncles, my cousin Bobby Hinson and my brat brother Chris. Grandma floats the white-icinged cake out from the kitchen, candles shaped into thirty-four and burning. Everybody belts out "Happy Birthday to You." The candles drip and Mama and Daddy smile uncommon.

Until Mama leans into the blow of thirty-four candles, jumping the fire into her wig. She yanks the blonde wig off to reveal her baldheadedness to a family crowd. She blows out a broken-winded scream and grabs her head. Daddy cusses. Grandma stomps to the kitchen with the wig. Aunt Camellia shoots the whole circus of us in Polaroid.

"Praise the Lord," Grandma Fleeta says, dropping the sizzling wig into dishwater. It snaps and pops into nothing. Mama flies upstairs sobbing. Daddy pours himself a jam-panic bourbon to the top of the glass. He jaw-locks his face, Brill-cream hair dark with fingers snaking through its thickness.

It reminds me of the sunrise after the first night Daddy stayed away from home all night. I had eaten cereal and fed bratty Chris and kissed Mama good-bye, like this could not be anything but normal. Mama had waited up late playing their solid favorite record, Herb Alpert, that they jitterbugged to. Mama spun that record over and over, staring out the den window. Finally she ran to the stereo, lifted the needle arm up, and hooked it down. She said not one word, but padded to the bedroom and shut the door. I had turned off the stereo spin.

Now Daddy's up-ended the glass, emptied the bourbon down. He grabs his hat and coat to head into the December chill of north Florida fog. But first, he holds his hands out for Uncle Eugene's keys.

"Where you going, Bo, darling?" Grandma Fleeta says.

"Smokes," Daddy says.

Cousin Bobby kicks up from the table and passes me to push out the back door. He shoots baskets with a rotting tether ball in the fog-scabby backyard. Why I don't know but a crush on him has fallen big over me. He plays star, a running back for Havana High School football. I'm just punky in eighth grade, fish-faced, buck-teethed, freckled. This summer at the town pool, Bobby strained to stare at my growing chest every day. Tonight, he's told me, everybody meets at Canny's Shack. Sneak out. One a.m. Bring Buffalo Punch.

Now I see from my eye corners Aunt Camellia signaling to Grandma in a throat-slit sign that No, she won't volunteer to check on Mama. She points to me and Chris with an eyebrow raise, shakes her head No, aims her pointer at Grandma Fleeta.

"Take this stuff to the kitchen, Lu Ellen, Hon," Grandma Fleeta says to me. She hands over two chicken and potato sticky plates. Bratty Chris is yanking the cat's tail, so I kick him swift in the butt.

"The good Lord knows how hard he tried, Camellia," Grandma Fleeta says as they clack dishes. "They say it's her hormones makes her act crazy. Can't say as I blame the boy. My boy. And boys will be boys."

By hormones, Grandma means Mama screaming, losing her hair, running away some nights, ever since the first time Daddy stayed away all night. Doctors said hormones and nerves. By boys, Grandma means Daddy drinking and borrowing Uncle Eugene's keys to meet his girl-friend at Eugene's Bar.

"Taking the children with you, Bo?" Grandma hollers, spilling the question out the door towards Daddy. But he's already just a fog figure swallowed up in night, walking the long grass drive to his jeep.

I leap two at a time steps to check on Mama. The door she's clicked locked.

"It's me," I say, so she unclicks the lock. The wood-walled farm-house room is painted ruint-white. Before he died, Grandpa had plas-tered an archway between the bedroom and bathroom vanity. Mama flops down before the mirror. I walk in and smell burnt fake hair and pink and purple shell soaps set in bowls of lion claws. Chris and I are not allowed to touch this clean soap with our filthy hands, Grandma has said.

"Come here," Mama says and scrapes me into her lap, pats my hair. Sun glasses off, she's splashed blue eye shadow on to set off her eyes. Sprigs of dark blonde and some gray hair stubs crack through her scalp. She looks pretty, even bald. "You're so beautiful and young," she says. "I'm just a bald old woman." She lip bites it out so I know she will shake her way out for one of her wild nights drinking and getting with men she does not know. Sometimes, she's out all night, but most are macaroni-and-cheese nights sitting with me and bratty Chris. Some-times we play Monopoly or cards in the TV room or talk. Always sad-ness and restlessness mix together in her green eyes. I know when I leave this room, she'll make a trail to home and dig up another wig and press on more makeup.

I turn to Mama and hug her hard. "You're beautiful, Mama, and not old," I say, climbing off her lap and heading downstairs to check on Chris.

Two hours pass and when Daddy nor Mama appear, Aunt Camellia pitches herself upstairs with a dinner knife to check on Mama. Aunt Camellia blams the door open and then slams it shut. She sways back down the stairs; she starts packing up pots and pans to go.

"Jesus Christmas, Mom," Aunt Camellia says to Grandma. "I know exactly where *she* is, exactly where *he* is. This is the absolute pits." Uncle Eugene and Cousin Bobby warm up the car to leave what remains of Grandma Fleeta's Coon Bottom, Florida farm. They're headed to Havana, a two-lane ride through tobacco field road. I slink into the kitchen where Aunt Camellia is hollering. "Do they take us for fools? They're both selfish as hell." With that, she notices me stealing in and points to me and Chris in the dining room and signals the cut-throat head shake of No, thinking I do not see the sign that she will not take my brat brother Chris and me home with her. Our house lies due north one mile over dirt roads towards Georgia.

"Now you shush up, Camellia Jane Phelps Hinson, you don't know—"

"Oh, cut the crap, Mom," Aunt Camellia says.

"You must stop taking God's name in vain and using vulgar expletives in this—"

"That's enough," Aunt Camellia says, disappearing with her pots into the night.

Grandma Fleeta cries herself a good one and heaps chocolate cake onto her plate. She eats. Chris strings licorice into his shoelace holes, and eats what breaks off along the way. My stomach sloshes sickish.

"I'm kinda feeling sick," Chris says.

"Oh, shush up, you're just begging for attention," I say. Then he throws up on Grandma's smushed up rug and the cat's tail. This gives

Grandma something to fuss over. She throws Chris into her arms and darts off to the medicine cabinet of her bedroom's bathroom.

This affords me the opportunity to sneak into Grandma's liquor cabinet to search out Buffalo Punch makings. Since everybody is sneaking out tonight, I play a killing sweet smile to Grandma when she comes out of her bedroom.

"Your brother's asleep in my room, so don't go waking him up," Grandma says, her brow sweat beading. I pretend to go to bed in the room where Mama cried at the mirror. I pull on Bobby's old pj's and say 'Now I Lay Me Down to Sleep' for Grandma. I ask her to tuck me in.

At eleven, the phone rings and Grandma answers it downstairs. "No, the kids are fast asleep and don't know a thing," she says. "We've got to find them . . .don't you *dare* call the police, Camellia. That would bring disgrace to the Phelps name. Now get to bed. The kids will be fine. . . . Yep, sound asleep."

She slams the phone down. The sofa's rusting springs bark as she lies down to watch TV. Soon she begins to snore. I grab the keys to Mama's car and tiptoe back into the kitchen's liquor cabinet. Buffalo Punch means everything. Everything alcohol, everything punch. Grandma Fleeta's cabinet offers only cooking sherry and canned orange juice. I tuck them under my arm and glide down the road to Mama's station wagon. She never drives when she goes hormonal. Grandma will not even hear the start up of car.

The moon hangs one night past full in the foggy night. The fallow fields blue and wetten as I drive the highway to Canny's abandoned shack. Nobody ever enters the shack. The roof might cave in.

My cousin Bobby is dancing and in charge of the Buffalo Punch. Everybody has poured Kool-Aid and vodka, cherry Coke and Jack Daniels, cooking sherry and orange juice into the ice chest of Styrofoam. Bobby scoops drinks out with a paper cup into Coke bottles, school Thermoses and flower vases, anything to disguise Buffalo punch from the showing up of police.

Carla Stallings, who possesses the Playbunniest body in ninth grade, starts dancing to somebody's Chevrolet radio music. She waves her long hair around in the car headlights, and does eye-closed gyrations. Then she strips to bra and underwear. Kelsey Hellman and Cindy Dalton stand around drinking down punch. And Sammy Stalworth and Pete Morgan. And kids from my class. They start up spin-the-bottle.

High school cheerleaders and guys already out of high school check in to the party. After two Buffalo punches drunk from the label peeled sherry bottle, I feel I can fly or my hair might fly off. I begin to dance in headlights beside Carla.

"See ya," Carla says, and tackles Sammy Stalworth. The air is a haze of ocean and next thing I know they are rolling around the ground making out. Some sudden body shouts "Okay, everybody strip!" Herds of people leap around the December chill fog in underwear.

I strip, too, and Peter Morgan catches up to me, lays an arm around my shoulder. I share my Buffalo punch. Next thing I know, Ugh, we're making out. French kissing. I think of wet caterpillars jumping into your mouth and jumping out again. I scope the party. French kissing is everybody. I wonder if Sammy or Bobby technique their French kisses less fishy. Or the boys not in high school. So in my wonderment, I kiss every boy at Canny's abandoned shack.

I'm kissing a boy I do not even know and he kisses not so great as a lizard might, and he starts leg rubbing hard on me. I shake him away and he says "Please." We kiss more and drink more punch and he starts rubbing hard on my leg again. Before I can shove him away, he barfs. Lucky it's not on me.

I get underwater dizzy and barely put one leg in front of another. The world swirls straight out in front of me, but it twists backwards around the outer edges of my eyes. I find cousin Bobby and start crying and telling him the older boy was using me. Bobby stares at my boobs and I remember I'm wearing a bra only on top. I start to chill in goosebumps and then I forget what happens next, except somebody feels me up and I keep on crying.

Carla is weeping because she's lost her underwear. She's barfed all over them and taken them off, she says, and now cannot find her clothes.

Now all of a split second sudden, I am sitting behind the wheel of Mama's car driving the wrong lane, trying to get back to Grandma Fleeta's. A weak pink and yellow light peeks up over the tobacco fields. "Just get back to Grandma's," I am saying, "Please dear God, just let me get back."

Then I see Mama. Slant-walking along the road. Hobbling. Her new wig, a black one that flips up on the ends, sits sideways. As I get closer, I see she wears one high heel only and the other foot bare. I pull over and see mascara black smeared all down her face. I barf and she cries.

Mama takes the car keys and we head to the 7-Eleven where they stay open always. Mama waits till they brew coffee fresh, and wipes the mascara smeared down her face with a McDonald's napkin fished from the glove compartment. I sneeze four times together. I say thank goodness at least I remembered my clothes, to myself in secret. Mama swings out the door and hands over a cup of coffee and blows the surface of hers. My first cup of coffee. It splashes bitter on my tongue and throat, even with a tear-open sugar packet. We sit in the parking lot a fair while, slurping coffee, staring off through the highway.

Then she says, "We're up shit creek without a paddle, you know." She darts a shy look over at me. "You know, in trouble." She muscles her mouth up a the ends like a closed mouth smile. "Did you have a fun time tonight?" she says.

"Not really," I say.

"I know," she says. "Me, either."

"Daddy's affair is killing me," she says. A car whiz-roars by on the highway. "Sometimes I just can't help myself." She looks into her coffee. "Sometimes I just need a change of scenery on the man front. Do you know what I mean?"

Now I know. She'll go home, Daddy'll go home, and brat brother Chris and I will stay over with Grandma Fleeta again. Tomorrow Mama will buzz us off home and everything there will act balanced like no blood wildness ever happens. Except the black fly shadow of it will hang in the house corners, a house so stiffed-up old nobody wants to go in, like Canny's shack.

"Uh-huh," I say.

"Thanks for understanding," Mama says, wrapping her naked warm fingers around my wrist. "I'm lucky I've got such a beautiful daughter," she says. "I mean it, Lu Ellen."

As we throttle our way up Grandma Fleeta's driveway, she says, "Tell your Grandma your Daddy's safe. And I'm safe. And you have her fix you a good breakfast, you and Chris." I sneeze another four in a row and nod. "And some fresh orange juice," she says. "And drink a Coke with aspirin so your head won't hurt so bad all day."

When I shut the car door, she vrooms off. The tail lights draw a slide of red through yellow-brown morning. I can see Mama's silhouette. The wig sits still lopsided on her head. I start to run after the car to knock on the window and say something. *Take me with you.* But no. I don't want to go. The red lights paint a C, turn right, and head home, so I swerve and aim up the drive to Grandma's.

Bring Buffalo Punch, cousin Bobby'd said. Like hell, I think, spitting the coffee tang off my tongue. I stumble up the drive and stare out at the fallow fields, the earth's deadened heart turned over and over into chaw and cigar and flakes of smoke tobacco.

Someday I will fly off, but not like hair flying off. I climb the steps dizzy as a wobbly wig and open the door to the smell of rhubarb and strawberry pie homemade and finally feel a warm soak towards my bones. When I leave someday, I'll fly in a car with red lights, whiz-roaring through the highway. And I won't check the rearview mirror for a long long time. For now, though, I'm sinking slow like a down mattress, lowered into spending another day at Grandma Fleeta's acres of home and the taste of pie. I will have some for breakfast, its sweet-sour deliciousness together. Sometimes a body needs the smell of rhubarb and strawberries baking.

ONE-FORTY-FOUR

I admit I persuaded Janine to sneak off that Saturday night, but I had no idea what waves of heat baked in her. It started on Thursday as we stood, thumbs out, at the drive-in where "Cotton Pickin' Chicken Pickers" was featured. Of course cars buzzed past fast and didn't stop. I asked Janine what she thought about Madalyn Murray O'Hair, the there's-no-god lady, and no angels, no heaven, no hell. Janine glanced her you're-so-dumb-I-wonder-why-we're-friends look.

"Fredda Kay, you ask the weirdest questions. I don't know. I guess she's kookoo," Janine said, thumb out as a VW bug pistol-fired its tin drum engine past. She wiped her forehead. The August heat from the Tallahassee tar road melted us down. But she cocked her head and stared serious a minute. "There's a hell, anyway."

We gave up getting a ride and laid our towels inside the tarry marquis entrance to sun ourselves. Ninety-five degrees and the sun jutted into us, me hoping deodorant swallowed smell. Four boys pulled over in a roar and grunt white Fairlane. The car vibrated with loudness.

"Yuk, Rickards Rednecks," Janine said, sitting up on elbows. Most Leon High boys would never drive Fairlanes. Most Cobb Jr. High kids would move over to Leon after ninth grade. Leon was the desirable school, but Janine and I both lived near Rickards, so we dreaded our move next year. Godby lined up next, but the mixed up newness of it made it questionable and way across town. Rickards—the worst. Their mascot was named Redskin, so Leon called them Rickards Rednecks. Thanks to my parents' divorce, I'd belong to Rickards Rednecks.

"Hey, where you going?" said the boy driving. He'd sweated a lot or hadn't washed his hair in three weeks.

"Nowhere," said Janine. "We're just laying here getting some sun. Bye." She laid down. Janine got rid of people she did not want to fool with. The driver shrugged, the Fairlane roared off.

"Rickards Rednecks, one hundred and forty-four," Janine said. In eighth grade math we learned that the number one hundred forty-four made a gross, so we secret-coded one-forty-four when we meant gross, as in socially unacceptable, reject, pariah.

"I'll be at Rickards in another year, that's one-forty-four," I said. Daddy was a Tucker. Mama and I lost everything when they divorced. Daddy's daddy set us up in a rental stucco house to keep things quiet. Granddaddy looked out after things, like when Daddy bit the end of a guy's ear off in the bar fight. Bailed Daddy out of jail, paid for that guy to get a fake ear, which kept the whole business out of court.

No favor, that, moving us to the stucco house of smudgy walls and dog-bathing Lysol smell that never quite dried out. The house sat smack in the center of the Rickards school district. We lost the big white country house and I lost my old horse, Princess. Now, I owned a homemade skateboard, a squeaky bed and a faded chenille bedspread in a wall-cracked bedroom. I wanted an orange-daisied bedspread, but Mama said to save up for it. If we lived with Daddy, Mama and I would have driven to the department store, picked out a bedspread, curtains to match. I smeared sweat from my face.

"Damn, it's hot," Janine said. "Wish I brought Coke money." She lived just this side of wrong in the Rickards-Leon line, in a newer neighborhood. She said her daddy's connections could get her into Leon. Janine lived modern in one-story with an automatic dishwasher, tan carpet, fern-green walls. White furniture perched in the living room.

"Hey, how y'all doing?" a voice punctuated beside us. I looked up. Two guys in a blue Roadrunner. They'd pulled in the drive-in exit side and peeked over the sign at us. The one who'd sat on the passenger side said, "I'm Jerry, and this is Dave." Jerry's teeth bucked out and his arms jangled skinny around him. Dave, the blonde Beatle-haired driver, stared blue-eyed and who-cares-if-they-answer-or-not at us. This made him extra attractive.

"Y'all go to Cobb or Raa?" said Jerry, the skinny one.

"*Cobb*," Janine said, flicking her satin blonde hair around, like how could he not know this? It put her out that they caught on to our only-in-junior highness. We stood and walked over. Dave talked to Janine right away, staring at her hair and cheerleader legs while she leaned a hip sway back and forth, playing with her hair, blowing pink bubbles of gum. I coasted around to Jerry's side of the car. I could tell that when he stood, his arms'd stretch and jangle way on past his knees.

They went to Rickards, and said It's not so bad. I wondered would I meet them if I lived in the country white house. Sometimes living close to town exploded my world into a bigger thing. Janine and I could catch the bus to town, and when we walked down Magnolia Drive, people we knew drove by and honked. In the country, no one my age had lived near, so I had talked to Princess instead.

Jerry told me you could skip easy in high school and leave for lunch. I told him I decided to take Art not Business Skills for ninth grade elective, and he said Why do that, you already took Art or Chorus in eighth grade, didn't you?

"Fredda Kay's got this new idea she's gonna go to college and be an *artist*," Janine said. She laughed like a long ache that fell into my belly. Dave said Knock it off, art was cool, if that's what I wanted. He talked about the new Rickards art teacher, young and miniskirt-wearing. We asked about school dances and PE and asinine teachers and where to smoke cigarettes. Then Jerry asked us to meet them at the 7-Eleven on Magnolia Drive that Saturday night. I told Jerry Okay. I reasoned that Janine would hitch up with Dave and I could look at him. He acted seventeen, and his long blonde lashes curled girlish.

"Hey, they're older, and they can drive," I said to Janine by phone late that night. I'd put the fan three feet away and turned it on full whir. Sweat drops coasted down my neck and we whispered; we could both get restrictions for late talking on the phone. "That makes up for them being Rickards Rednecks, doesn't it?" She didn't answer. "Well, doesn't it?" I whispered again, louder. Her silence spit hysterical through phone static.

"I don't know. I guess," Janine said, in her throw-up voice. Janine feared weirdly of throwing up in public places. Once in eighth grade Math class, she sent a note commanding me to not tell anyone, but what if she threw up right now in class? She'd flatten into embarrassment, she'd never face school again. I'd glanced her over. She clutched her stomach and turned wired up white. After that, she had asked Mr. Munroe to change her seat to by the door.

"But don't tell anybody at Cobb that we're going to meet Rickards Rednecks, okay?" Janine said. "Nobody. Swear. On a stack of bibles. And whatever you do, don't ever tell my parents." But I already knew Dave pushed past redneck. That day, after he'd got his fill of Janine's hair and legs, he'd watched and listened while the rest of us talked. Before we said bye, he'd called Janine poor little rich girl. She dressed in expensive Hang Ten clothes, but her daddy wouldn't allow her dates till she'd turned sixteen. Her parents gave her a stereo, but they never turned her loose except to my house, and they didn't trust Mama.

I secretly fell in hard love with Dave, but I knew I could not touch that idea. He and Janine made a snappy couple, both TV cute. Jerry was scrappy, but ugly as homemade sin. That's what my Great Aunt Agatha had said about my Indian grandmama who I'd never seen; birthing my daddy, she'd died. Aunt Agatha prided herself on her tiny waist. She'd called my grandmama thick-waisted and big boned and big nostriled. Homely described Jerry, but I could tolerate him.

On Saturday afternoon, Janine came over and flung herself and her light green makeup case down on my bed. "Damn, this bed is loud," she said. "And it's too hot to be alive. Ninety-nine degrees. I called time-temperature before I left." She stared at the ceiling a while and then sat up. "Hey, try on your new pantsuit for me."

I put the jumpsuit on. I was embarrassed to wear clothes Mama made. We couldn't afford Villager dresses like popular girls wore, and it felt like broadcasting to wear homemade. But this pantsuit—fluorescent lime green polyester—had a vest chaining a gold button across it. The pants flared into floaty bell bottoms.

"It looks great," she said. I rolled my eyes. I looked in the mirror. Coarse and curling black hair, big Indian nose. Janine stood behind me in the mirror, four inches taller, skinnier hips, satin blonde hair she'd curled the ends of. I winced at my clown suit look.

"Come on, Janine, it doesn't look great," I said, yanking the ends of my hair. "I just hope it doesn't make me look fat. Can you roll my hair tonight so it'll wave just on the ends?"

"I like it curly like that, it's so shiny. Why don't you just let it do what it wants?" she said, combing her fingers through her own satiny strands. Her hair waved at the ends when it got hot and humid. Mine frizzed.

"Cause it's a hundred and forty-four," I said.

"Okay, after we get home from the 7-Eleven." That polyester pantsuit sweated and itched me hard, so I peeled it off fast. I pulled on my shorts.

Janine stood, shut the door, tiptoed back to the bed.

"Let's raid your mama's liquor cabinet," she whispered.

"I don't know about that, Janine. Why don't we ask her? She'll let us." Even though Mama came home work-tired, plunked in front of the TV and stared, and even though she listened to Andy Williams songs like "Moon River" and "Chestnuts Roasting on an Open Fire," she could be called pretty cool. She'd told me I could have a drink with her any time I wanted.

"No way," Janine said. "She'll say no. And even if she does say yes, she'll tell my parents, and I'll be up the creek. I'll get slapped with restrictions the rest of my life." She had a point. Every time we turned around, her parents snooped around and caught us doing stuff.

Every Saturday when we went to the two o'clock matinee, Janine's dad's car was parked across Main Street. He read the newspaper behind the wheel, like he could hide. If we planned to meet guys, we instructed them to head upstairs, last row of the balcony. Sometimes we didn't care about the movie, so we'd pay, walk inside, and hand our tickets to tear in half. We'd go straight to the bathroom, put on frosted lipstick, watching my Timex. Ten minutes after the show started, Mr. Whatley's car disappeared. We'd count to two hundred, then head outside, turn left, cut down the stinky alley that led to Park Avenue. We'd meet the guys by the police station. When no guys belonged in the plan, we walked to Woolworth's to flip through records and order a double banana split. I had no idea yet that Mr. Whatley got more strange.

"Okay, we'll sneak into the liquor cabinet," I said. "But if you get caught, tell them it was your idea. They hate me already. They think I'm the one who gets you in trouble. Remember when we skipped school because you got a ride with Timmy to the beach? They blamed me, remember? It was your idea."

"Okay, okay, but we won't get caught," she said.

That night Mama savored a couple of bourbon and Cokes, mopped her forehead and said, "I wish we had one of those room air conditioners. The heat's got me beat, girls, I'm going to bed." On the TV news, Daddy's mug had appeared in the local briefs because he invested in the richest neighborhood yet; he broke ground for his house there. Things like that exhausted my mother.

So after Janine and I watched *Star Trek*, we opened the kitchen cabinet under the sink, and grabbed out the bourbon and the vodka. Janine opened the bourbon bottle and lifted it to her mouth. She turned it up, the liquid swishing down to her mouth. She swigged two big ones. The vodka rested by her hip.

"Gyah, that's gross," she said, coughing into her arm so Mama wouldn't hear. We said gyah so we wouldn't have to say God, taking the Lord's name in vain. Girls said other things instead of cussing. Like my grandmother said "Dod Limit" instead of god damn it. I'd realized females all talked in a code, because the world thought the truth was too hard for girls.

I took a slow swig of bourbon. It tasted like poison, and felt like somebody burned a birthday candle in my throat.

"One hundred and forty-four!" I said, handing her the brown liquor bottle.

"No, you hold this one," she said, handing it back as the amber liquid swooshed in the bottle. She pulled the top off the cheap vodka. "I'm trying this one. Aren't you supposed to swallow worms and eat a lemon with this stuff?"

"No, I think that's tequila. Shh, Mama will hear us," I said.

"Holy shit," she said after the vodka. "I think I'm going to throw up. You want some?" I shook my head no, and drank some more bourbon. We sat a while taking chugs, coughing and shuddering, not saying much, the smell of liquor smudging the air between us. "Ready to face the Rickards Rednecks?" she said.

"Yeah," I said. "Dave's cute. He's not a real redneck, is he?" Janine shrugged. "Maybe we'll even pass them if we go down JimBo Road," I said, and I tumbled down another swallow of bourbon. I stood up. Janine took another big gulp of vodka, then another bourbon, and coughed. I spun my way to the bedroom to get our loafers. We had drunk four inches down, so Janine filled the bottles back up with water. I felt like I bubbled across the house. I pulled my loafers on, and handed Janine hers.

"Should we change?" Janine said, shoving the bottles in the cabinet. "My mama says ladies shouldn't wear shorts, especially after dark and outside." I couldn't believe so-wild Janine would care about shorts-wearing. Besides, her mama faked this act for her social friends at the country club like she did not smoke and did come from money. When she arrived home, she chain smoked all day, and Janine herself told me her mama grew up trailer trash. Once I saw Mrs. Whatley in the bedroom watching *The Guiding Light* while she ironed, cigarette in one hand, iron in the other. And the ashtray brimmed over with butts and ashes.

"Your mama's full of shit," I said. It spilled out of me. "I mean, don't worry about it, Janine. What do you think? Somebody's gonna rape us? Fat chance."

"Okay," she said, "but Mama said if you wear shorts at night, you're just asking for it."

"Well, my mama says dress however you want, but remember chameleons," I said. I locked the door and dropped the key in my shorts pocket. "Dress to protect yourself."

"What're you talking about?" she said, tumbling down the drive.

"Well, like if we were outside running in our underwear, it might be different. Use your noggin, my mama says. You can't just say 'Girls shouldn't wear shorts at night.' It depends."

"Fredda Kay, sometimes you talk so serious and weird," she said squealing a laugh. "I don't know what the hell you're talking about."

"Nothing," I said. "Never mind. Janine, you're drunk."

"Look who's talking," she said as I tripped at the end of the driveway and nearly fell on the street.

We walked down Magnolia Drive to long JimBo Road that led to Rickards. The air had cooled. We ran, in case liquor was loaded with calories and fattened you. We ran five blocks, then turned down the backside of my neighborhood by the duck pond, back uphill to Magnolia Drive. We huffed and pumped and snorted at the top of the hill. We pulled our sticky shirts from our skin. We stood dizzy and stuck.

"We don't have money for the 7-Eleven," Janine said.

"Who cares," I said. "We'll see Dave and Jerry there." The older kids hung out there, since this clerk sometimes sold them beer.

"Let's try to get somebody to buy us a beer," Janine said. We panted to 7-Eleven, blowing our shirts dry. Some of the popular Leon kids hung out in a Mustang convertible to the darkened right side of the lot. A couple made out in the back seat, and others stood around doing a restless shift and talk. By the newspaper stand stood popular Cobb kids, like goodie Paula Moore.

"Pop Tarts," I said.

"Come on," Janine said, "let's go talk to them."

"Hey there," said Paula, fake. She didn't know our names, but acted gushy; still, she stared at our short shorts. She wore a pair of culottes. "What are y'all doing up here?"

"We got drunk," Janine bragged. "We stole some liquor from Fredda Kay's mom's liquor cabinet and sneaked out." Inside I cringed. How much did you tell people, especially gossipy pop-tarts, about things risky? Once Toni Underwood had come to school on a Monday bragging about getting drunk with a high school boy and driving down to Blue Sink where nice girls didn't go. By sixth period, the whole school was calling her a whore.

"Oh, wow, lucky you," said Paula's boyfriend, Mitchell. He wore his usual student-council white shirt and navy pants. I watched him study Janine with interest, like he'd never noticed her before.

"How'd you guys get here?" Janine said.

"I ride around with my brother when he's not dating somebody," Mitchell said. "He lets me come along if I do his weekend paper route, and if I stay away from the car. Sometimes he gives me a beer."

"Lucky," Janine said. We packed in close and talked about how relieved we were not to ever sit through Mrs. Derrell's eighth grade English class again, how we hated diagramming sentences. How we memorized gross poems like "I think that I shall never see, a poem lovely as a tree." I told them I memorized it to "In-A-Gadda-Da-Vida," and I started to sing it for them until Paula looked at me like she would croak.

"I'm on the annual staff," Mitchell said, "and did you know—*Jennifer Jackson* got nominated by the teachers last year for Miss Eighth Grader? A colored person." Everybody groaned. Everybody but me. Even though my blood surged warm and floaty in my face and fingers, I sobered and scared down quiet.

"So?" I said. They all turned and looked at me. Jennifer Jackson turned me into an A and out of a C in pre-algebra. Out in the hallway whenever Mr. Munroe gave us permission for her to lend me special help. "She's nice," I said weakly. "Smart." We had started telling knock-knock jokes and laughing so hard, we'd tear outside to laugh out loud when they got really stupid. "And funny." *Jennifer Jackson is my friend*, I did not say. But if I did, it might bring attention to my brownish part-Seminole skin and hair. They might call me bad names. One forty-four or worse. So I clinked my back to the brick wall breathing bullet blue and red-aching white in my stomach. I hated Pop Tart kids. And more, myself. Couldn't I say Jennifer Jackson is my friend?

Jerry and Dave drove up in the Roadrunner. Everybody turned around to look at its loudness. "Rickards Rednecks," said Mitchell. Jerry and Dave waved, and I waved back. Janine acted like she didn't know them. She turned her back to the roadrunner and faced Mitchell and Paula.

"Oh, Janine, your hot pants are triple-O cool," Paula was saying. Relieved, I padded over to Jerry and leaned in to look at Dave's long eyelashes.

"Hey, guys," I said. "We got drunk tonight, me and Janine. We raided my mother's liquor cabinet. Bourbon and vodka."

"That's cool," Jerry said. His teeth bucked bad. Jangly arms. I couldn't act a triple-O cool crush on him. "Why doesn't Janine come over here?" he said. "Is she stuck up or something?"

Dave stared straight at Janine, then turned back to me. You couldn't guess what he was thinking. I liked that, a mystery movie guy. I walked around the back of the car to the driver's side. I counted five freckles on his nose and cheeks. Gyah, the perfect number of freckles.

"So what y'all been doing?" I said.

"Just riding around," Jerry said. "Went out to Blue Sink. Got my cousin to buy us some beer. Want one?"

Jerry reached across Dave's face to hand me a beer, but I shook my head no.

"Wait till Janine gets here and we get in the car," I said. "You never know who might see us."

"You got an overactive imagination," David said, smiling. Mitchell and Paula left in the Mustang with Mitchell's brother. Janine stood with her back to us, like fascinated by the "ICEES Small—10 cents, Medium—15 cents, Super—25 cents" sign in the window. She waited by the newspaper bin till the Mustang disappeared. Then she wandered over to the Roadrunner. "So the poor little rich girl got drunk tonight," Dave said. Janine paled and breathed fast. Dave handed us each a Busch Bavarian.

"Yeah," she said. Dave and Janine climbed into the back seat. I sat behind the wheel, Jerry beside me.

"Hey, Dave," I asked, "please let me drive." I glanced into the rear-view window. "Just down to the elementary school, circle around and back here."

"Okay, what the hell," he said. My heart beat fast as a sharp radio song. My fingers on the keys, beer can cool between my thighs, my right foot planted on the accelerator and the left on the clutch. In the rearview mirror, I could see Janine and Dave making out.

Suddenly, Janine's daddy's face hung beside my window outside the car. His hair stuck up, his eyes unfocussed. Talk about drunk. "Janine, get out of that car," he said. "I want to talk to you, young lady."

"Shit, where'd he come from?" Jerry whispered.

"Shit, shit, shit," Janine said. "Oh, shit." We all quieted and let her out. She kicked a beer bottle out onto the pavement, and it rolled and clinked down toward the street.

"Holy Shit," Dave whispered. But her daddy didn't notice. Wine or steak juice, something dark had spilled on his white dress shirt. He grabbed her elbow and led her up the hill where the Office Lounge was. We called it the Fice Lounge since the O had fallen off the sign. How stupid of us to walk up Magnolia Street, exactly the way Janine's parents drove home from the country club every Saturday night after they dined there. He saw her, walking to or standing at the 7-Eleven, and drove back after he dropped Mrs. Whatley home.

"What do you think he'll do to her?" Jerry said.

"I don't know," I said, peeling the label off my beer bottle. "What should I do?"

"Nothing to do but wait," Dave said. I tried to not fall to disappointed about not driving. I sipped beer and tried to think of something to get off the subject.

"Do you guys play sports?" I asked.

"Basketball," Dave said. "Football's for small brainers." Jerry said he played junior varsity, but Dave played varsity. I promised I'd come watch games when basketball season came, then asked them if high school was better than junior high. "Of course," Dave said.

"We get to leave thirty-five minutes every day if we want," Jerry said.

"How lucky," I said, hearing the fade in my own voice. I slurped beer. My stomach frothed and sloshed hot. "How does that thing go?" I said. "Whiskey on beer, have no fear—"

"Beer on whiskey, mighty risky, whiskey on beer, have no fear," said Dave. "It's the other way around, but the same thing. That means you screwed up, Fredda Kay." I already burned from confusion without him reminding me.

"You gave me the damn beer, Dave," I said turning around and kneeling in the seat to give him the eyeball. "Contributing to the delinquency, you know. And you're delinquent, too."

"Hey, what's it with you?" he said. He'd decided to take his frustration out on me. "Don't you care what those Pop Tarts think? Or are you just drunk?" And what's the deal with your friend's father, anyway?"

His look felt like he'd slashed a hole in my chest. I didn't answer. I did care, I didn't care. I didn't know what I thought about anything. His long eyelashes killed me. I turned around and sat.

"What's taking them so long?" I said. "I'm gonna find out." I pushed open the squeaky door of the Roadrunner. I walked up the steep hill through the kudzu where I spotted Janine's daddy's Oldsmobile parked facing the Sears Shopping Center, away from me. The windows were rolled down. Then I dead stopped.

In the streetlight I saw him lean over to her side of the car. She leaned way far out the window, moving away. He tried to stroke her hair. My legs cheated me and started to give. I backed up and headed down the hill. Jerry and Dave smoked cigarettes in the car. I couldn't tell them. Girls had to always code talk, and I sure couldn't tell this.

I had to rescue her. I ran back up the hill and stood in the light about five cars away so they couldn't tell that I'd seen them. I started yelling, "Janine! Janine! Where are you? We've got to go home. Right now. Where are you? Janine?"

She jumped out of the car and stood, leaning on the door. My legs could hardly walk over to her. She tried to slow down her breathing and swallow. She straightened up but held her hands flat against the car door like she tried to hold something inside.

"Right here, Fredda Kay. Daddy'll drive us back to your house, okay?" Janine said.

"But Jerry and Dave said they'd—"

"He doesn't want them to. He says I have to go home if I don't let him drive us," she said. Her voice shook.

"Oh. Well, let me go tell them bye," I said. She nodded. I raced through the Fice Lounge parking lot and down the hill through the kudzu. "Y'all go on," I said to the guys. "We have to let him take us home, or she's in deep shit."

"Poor little rich girl," Dave said, getting out to take the front seat.

"Call us tomorrow at my house, okay?" I said, and tore up the hill.

Mr. Whatley weaved in and out of the wrong lane all the way down Magnolia Street. Janine crawled in the back seat with me, and we scooted over to the right side in case he crashed into another car. I wondered if I should pretend I didn't see what I saw. When Mr. Whatley pulled up into my yard and let us out, he said, "Janine, you stay away from those boys, you hear me?" He tried to focus on me, and said, "They're trash."

"Yessir," she said. I unlocked the door and we flung ourselves inside. We changed into pajamas without glancing at each other. I wished I'd never seen a thing. Mama didn't wake up. We crawled into bed and turned our backs to the middle.

"Goodnight Janine," I said, faking a voice even.

"Goodnight," she said. Neither of us slept for hours, just listening to each other breathe. Janine hid things so well. I'd never remembered her to cry. She just got mad. I'd never bring it up, it would only cause trouble. But what if she needed help? When did a girl keep her trap shut and when did she talk? I made a pact with myself not to say anything forever, amen. I remembered her telling me what her mother had said: *If you wear shorts at night, you're just asking for it.* No wonder she didn't tell anybody.

But with this silence, I knew a big rock would wedge itself between us. I'd already done bad by Jennifer Johnson, I didn't want to screw up again in one night.

The next morning, Janine called her mother to come get her before breakfast. I watched her leave from the kitchen window.

"So, did you girls have a wild night?" Mama said. She'd walked into the kitchen and I hadn't noticed, but she took out the bourbon bottle now a weaker shade of amber and she chuckled. *Dress to protect yourself,* Mama had said. Who cared about new bedspreads and stereos, I had a mother who said, *It depends.* She weighed things, and I had to trust somebody.

"Mama," I began, "Remember you telling me about dressing like chameleons?" I didn't know where I'd go from here, but somehow, my words would get me there.

WHERE THE SHADOWS
TANGLE AND SNARE AND SING

Lazzie Mae lives in a shotgun house over at Smokey Holler. That's where the colored folks all have one-way-in and one-way-out houses that the sheriff owns. Lazzie Mae's mama works for my best friend Martha's family, the Thompsons.

Martha lives in a two-story brick house catty corner from Lazzie Mae's house. I love to go to the Thompson's house for two reasons. One, Martha owns her own canopy bed, and two, her daddy ministers at the First Presbyterian Church. He talks in church about things I do not understand. About old fear and despair and blood.

No, three reasons I like to stay at Martha's. The Thompsons live on the cliff above the railroad track, right across from Smokey Holler on the corner of Myers Park and Marvin Street. You can watch the action from the Thompson's screened in porch. One more reason. Cause Lazzie Mae gets to play with us when most kids don't get to play with colored children.

The Thompsons are what my daddy calls liberals. Martha's daddy stays home most of the time and he lets us squirt the hose and build mud houses on the street. My daddy stays home most of the time, too, but that's cause Mama's so sick and Daddy can't get a job. So they let me stay here a lot.

I love the view from the screen porch. Especially now, summer time. It's morning, when the colored women sweep their wood porches in the sizzling hot wearing washed-out house dresses; the trash piles burn. That's where Smokey Holler got named. It sits low below the waterfall line where the creek runs and the crematory burns the city trash. The smoke never rises too far off the ground and the wind does not blow through. The haze blues and blacks the whole neighborhood like old sad news.

Today Lazzie Mae's mama Ruth slumps in the chair shelling peas, and even with the fan on her and the shade trees underneath us, she keeps wiping sweat off her pretty face. Martha and Lazzie Mae and I crayon pictures of Lazzie Mae's one-way-in and one-way-out shotgun house. Martha colors it pink and blue and I color it purple and Lazzie Mae crayons it black and red.

"What's matter, Ruth?" Martha asks. Even if she is the preacher's kid, she's none too tactful. "Is Junior Brewster playing crazy again?"

"Pick that crayon up, girl, before it mashes into the concrete," Ruth says, sniffing. "Mind your own business while you at it."

"Not *playing* crazy," I say, "*plain* crazy. Is Junior Brewster plain crazy, Ruth?" Junior Brewster is Lazzie Mae's daddy and sometimes he gets real drunk and Ruth and Lazzie Mae bang on the Thompson's door late at night to spend the night, cause Ruth shakes her head and says, "He plain crazy tonight, Mr. Thompson." Other times Junior Brewster and Mr. Thompson work for what they call Civil Rights. Ruth's eyes turn sad and down to the ground those times, too.

"Mary and Martha, y'all can be quiet and mind y'alls own business," Lazzie Mae says. "Nosy girls."

Most times, though, she says she's proud of his working for the N-Double-A-C-P and for colored people to get on the front of the bus. Even though they go to the jailhouse. They moved the jailhouse right in the middle of Smokey Holler. One night last week, those men got so loud in the jailhouse singing and clapping and yelling they kept the close-packed neighborhood up till the dusty blue morning came peeping through.

The sheriff's deputy, Mr. Settlemeyer, told them to shut up or he'd set the jailhouse on fire. He was not lying. He had put the downtown jail to fire when the trouble started getting bad between coloreds and white. So he burned the jailhouse up and four colored people with it. The newspaper reported that the colored men in jail had set the fire by accident. Then the jail got moved down to Smokey Holler. Mr. Settlemeyer said 'Those niggers must be getting some kinda cocaine from that Martin Luther King fellow through the mail, cause no niggers would just keep singing and ignore those kinda threats.' He said this talk to my daddy down at the Last Chance Bar one afternoon when Mama sent me to fetch him.

"Who's that colored lady standing in the street, Ruth?" I ask. The lady's wearing long red petticoats and a black turban. Ruth does a double-take, then stands up stretching her neck.

"The Conjure Woman," she says, like I know who that is.

"What's the Conjure Woman?" Martha says. "Is she from the devil?" Conjure woman is waving her hands in the street facing Ruth's house.

"Oh, Lord," Ruth says.

"Who's that Conjure Woman, Ruth?" Martha says. "She run off Mr. Settlemeyer?"

"Hush up," Ruth says. "You girls full of the devilment. Now hush up."

That Mr. Settlemeyer reminds me of a panther. Got a lucky handsome face and squared jaw but yellow-green eyes you better not turn your back on. He sneaks around. Nighttimes off duty he sells moon-shine to the people of Smokey Holler, then arrests them for being drunk. I've seen him in the silky black night banging on Lazzie Mae's door and handing over the clear bottle to Junior Brewster. One night, that Mr. Settlemeyer talked a long time on the front porch to Ruth when Junior Brewster sat in jail.

I had heard Mr. Settlemeyer's voice raise up in a question, but I could hear fear and old bad news that night. Mr. Settlemeyer pulled on Ruth's arm when Junior Brewster was in the jailhouse and she pushed back and away and slammed the screen door and shut her big door even though the summer heat would cook up the house good with the door shut. Even though they didn't have screen in the windows and he could've climbed on in. She had shut the door in his face.

Sometimes Mr. and Mrs. Thompson and Ruth sit up late and talk murmuring low on the porch under Martha's room with the canopy bed. I know this because I have the hardest time sleeping on summer nights. They are the best times in the world. I get bubble-stomachy just looking at the smeary charcoal sky out to the west. You can look out Martha Thompson's high-up bedroom window and see the Florida state capitol building with the dome top and the confederate flag, the state flag and the flag of the United States waving above it all. And the train comes right by the house at nine-thirty and then at two in the morning. I love the metal rattle keeping its own time like the colored men who sing and scat on a Saturday afternoon, saying

Bwee dee da dee doom

Bwee dee de da doom.

Summertime, the sound of the adults murmuring low on the porch under Martha's room comes up like through the wisteria vines on the pine tree beside the house, winding its way up and around, twisting and turning and keeping on to the sky. They talk about grown up things, I guess liberal things like raising money to get people bailed out of jail, and sending money to the Reverend King and rounding up people to boycott the Florida Theatre downtown cause they won't let colored people in. They talk and it twists and turns, keeps to the sky like old news changing.

Now I've painted all my one-way-in and one-way-out shotgun house purple and now I got to paint the prancing horse on the screendoor and the cinderblocks the house sits up on. I'm deciding to color them yellow when I see that Junior Brewster's standing at the screen door between the Spanish bayonet plant and the plum tree next to the pine tree with the wisteria vine. He's wearing working clothes, blue pants on his blackish skin, sooty shoes for cleaning the capitol building with the big dome on top.

"What you doing here?" Ruth says. "Don't you see I'm working?"

"Hey, Daddy," Lazzie Mae says.

"What you doing here, Junior Brewster?" Martha says.

"I came to see you and say bye," Junior Brewster says. "Today we sit at the Bennett's Drugstore stools. Ask them to let us eat at the table."

"Oh, Lord," Ruth says.

"You aren't supposed to take the Lord's name in vain," Martha says.

"It's not vain. The who's-the-fairest-in-the-land queen in the fairy tale is vain," I say.

"Oh, Lord," Ruth says, standing up and setting her shelling peas on the chair. "I suppose I won't see you for a while." Ruth walks outside and they go across the street to the shotgun house.

"Oh, Jesus, he's going to jail again," Lazzie Mae says.

"You not supposed to take the Lord's name in vain," Martha says.

"That's not vain. The queen is vain," I say.

"Y'all can be quiet," Lazzie Mae says, sniffling.

"What you crying about, Lazzie Mae," Martha says.

"I ain't crying," Lazzie Mae says.

"Mind your own business," I say.

"You can be quiet, Mary," Martha says. I have a funny want to start crying myself. Soft. About the old sad news Mr. Thompson talks about. I sometimes know what he means. I can only feel it, like the colored men scatting on Saturday afternoon saying:

Bwee dee da dee doom

Bwee dee de da doom.

Like times my own daddy doesn't come home nights. Lazzie Mae tells me he's out jooking. I don't know what that means, but it makes my mama sigh sad and sick. It feels like needles press on the front of my eyes and I grit my teeth and hold on.

**

"Tonight's going to be dangerous," Mr. Thompson announces at dinner. This afternoon violent clouds burst their pewter curtains of rain on the black dirt. Before dinner and twilight, the fish-silver raindrops sparkled on the thick green leaves outside.

"Oh, Lordy," says Ruth, clearing dishes from the table.

"Daddy, people's not supposed to take the Lord's name in vain," Martha says.

"It's NOT vain," I say.

"I think I'd better fix a pallet on the kitchen floor for Lazarus Mae," Mrs. Thompson says. That's Lazzie's full name, Lazarus.

"Oh, Lord," Ruth says and we all get up from the table.

***

The pungent night air from the wet dirt outside falls around the house. Everybody who can glides off into sleep. I creep downstairs to get bedtime water and walk over to Lazzie Mae. I squat down. She looks at me.

"What?" she whispers, sitting up.

"I don't know," I whisper back. "I can't sleep at night in the summertime."

"Go on and mind your own business," she says, lying down. I pluck a kiss on her plum skin. She's pretty and bright-eyed like her mama and dark-skinned like her daddy and smells like smoke. She pushes me away and I tiptoe upstairs with my bedtime water.

I hear the chu-chung, chu-chung of the metal rattling on the train track outside. The train rumbles the whole house good and I think:

Bwee dee da dee doom

Bwee dee de da doom.

Then it is quiet until I hear from downstairs the sound that is not crying and is not singing coming up the dark stairs. It is the sound of old news. I lie still and cover my face since it might be a ghost or the Conjure Woman or my daddy.

****

The dogs start to barking first. Then the headlights on the dirt road below. The car motor runs like a fan around and around and around. It dies. Then the car door slams.

I hear the knock on the door downstairs. Martha takes in a deep breath and rolls over in her sleep and sighs. Nothing happens. The blood is bumping my heart in the back of my Adam's apple.

Another knock on the door downstairs. I see the yellow gold of light blink on under the door and I hear Mrs. Thompson murmuring. I hear Mr. Thompson padding down the hall, down the stairs and I creep into the hallway and squat at the top of the stairs.

"Mr. Thompson," says the Negro preacher man.

"Come in, Mr. Steele," says Mr. Thompson. Mr. Steele steps into the foyer, his hat off and jacket on in the dead of night and the sweat of summer.

"I don't mean to disturb your household, but they've got over a hundred men detained out at the fairgrounds this time. Too many to put into the jail," Mr. Steele says. He clears his throat. "Getting beaten with sticks and gun butts and I don't know what all. Junior Brewster's one who got it bad. Hit in the eye with Settlemeyer's backhand."

"I see. We'll have to get word to headquarters that we'll need some bail money," Mr. Thompson says. "Do we have anything in the account?"

"Not enough to get all these people out," Mr. Steele says. "They have no food, no indoor toilets, no water. And the beatings—"

"Yes, the beatings," Mr. Thompson says.

"Watch out for your neighborhood," Mr. Steele says. "And your back." He turns his back to the stairs and opens the door to the night with no mercy, like Mr. Thompson says in church. He disappears. I tiptoe back to Martha's bed and get in and wait for what's next.

*****

I hear the ghost downstairs, not crying and not singing. It's not like my daddy's voice drunk. I am dancing with the Conjure Lady in red petticoats and black turban. And then I am dancing with a big white hog bone, the blood meat still hanging off it.

I startle awake and I hear the dogs barking first. Then the headlights. And then the car like a fan running around and around and around. A car door slams in the frog and cricket night. I hear the not crying and not singing coming up the stairs. Martha is snoring. I tiptoe to the window. Mr. Settlemeyer. He's across the street banging on the door. Banging and banging on the door.

Martha wakes up when the dogs get louder. "What's that banging, Mary?" she says in half-awake talk.

"Get up and see," I say, waving her to the window. She stumbles out of bed in her long daddy t-shirt. We watch Mr. Settlemeyer in his uniform, his broad-brimmed hat, his gun at the ready in his leather holster. Banging on the door.

"What's he banging for?" Martha says.

"Come on downstairs," I say. "Let's go to the porch."

We tiptoe downstairs and find Lazzie Mae on the porch sitting in the swing looking through the haze of Smokey Holler square at her one-way-in and one-way-out shotgun house. Mr. Settlemeyer bangs again on the door.

"What's he banging for, Lazzie Mae?" Martha says.

"Getting what he wants," Lazzie Mae says.

Across the street, Ruth comes to the door in her shaggy old bathrobe hand-me-down terrycloth. She's grabbed it in the middle. Mr. Settlemeyer says something to her and she pushes him. He steps closer and pushes the screen door open. He pushes Ruth back into the house. Then he shuts the door where it will get to cooking in there. Lazzie Mae again starts up that sound that is not singing and is not crying.

"What you doing that for, Lazzie Mae?" Martha says.

"Mind your own business, Martha," I say.

"Why you taking her side, Mary?" Martha says.

"Hush up," Lazzie Mae says.

"I'm scared of the dark," Martha says.

"I'm scared for what happens in the dark," Lazzie Mae says.

"I'm scared," I say.

Seems like nothing is happening, but we're sitting on the porch, waiting all the same. Like at the creek down in the middle of Smokey Holler. It does not seem to be traveling at all and it seems to know nothing of the sea. But it moves just the same.

******

"What are you girls doing up?" Mr. Thompson says. We can hear the not crying and not singing across the street that woke him up.
"Mr. Settlemeyer just left from there," Martha says. "He went into Ruth's house and stayed for a long time."

"What are you girls doing up watching? Why didn't you wake me?" Mr. Thompson says.

"It would've happened just the same," Lazzie Mae says, watching Mr. Thompson put on his jacket and grab his hat to run across the street and see about Ruth.

"You girls all get on to bed," Mr. Thompson says.

"Daddy, we're scared," Martha says. "Did Mr. Settlemeyer hurt Ruth?"

"I want my mama," Lazzie Mae says, wailing now.

"Lazzie—Martha, take her on upstairs with y'all," Mr. Thompson says.

"She won't fit," Martha says.

"I'll get on the floor," I say.

"Now get on to bed," Mr. Thompson says.

****

Chu-chung, chu-chung, chu-chung, the two in the morning train goes. Lazzie Mae lies beside me, her hands behind her head, her eyes fixed on the canopy of the bed above. Martha sleeps on the floor. She's the only one who can sleep.

The train slows down and I think of the colored men scatting on Saturday afternoon,

Bwee dee da dee doom

Bwee dee de da doom.

The caboose whooshes by and the silence after comes oozing in the window.

The night finally cools, coming in the window, and I can smell the swamp at the bottom of the holler. The trash piles smells of smoke just beyond. I get up and go to the window and see the coal yard beyond the trash pile silhouetting black from gray. The moon stands silver as a picture frame in the sky. I look across the road to the house.

In the haze, I cannot quite make it out, but I know this sickness in my stomach is where the bad old lives, where Ruth's house sits, where the moonlight and the shadows tangle and snare and sing and cry out. Beyond the pine and plum tree and the twisty vines and the Spanish bayonet plant and crickets. Lazarus Mae gets up from bed to look out on the window with me.

"Your daddy is brave," I tell her. "And your mama is more brave." She looks over at me, and I see where her eyes hold the moon.

"I-I'm sorry," I murmur.

"Things changing," she says. She looks out onto what will be a sizzling hot morning, her eyes anchored up high on some news, new news I can't see, higher than the flags waving above us all.

RIGHT PAST THE PARTY

Misty's eye had grown so big the whites showed more than the brown as I'd led her around, walking and walking last night. Only cure for horse colic. But something crawled me, told me it was worse.

I'd spent nearly all night circling the pasture, and now the sunlight stabbed through the Spanish-style glass doors to my bedroom balcony. I drifted out of sleep, listening to Lily, who cleaned our house, chime out some old church song as she scrubbed the bathroom sinks. She had a thrilling singing voice that echoed through the house and hit my heart good. It helps a body through the day, singing to the Lord, she'd say. Helps a body's heart.

I smelled my browned sweaty hands, waiting for Mama to come bark me out of bed. Horses, the rich, sweet late summer hay scent I'd picked up patting Misty in the night as she sweat cold as a north Florida spring.

Even the vet had said he wasn't sure it was colic, and sent me to bed if she didn't improve in the next few hours. It could be heartworms, and, he said looking not at me, she might not pull through. I'd walked and walked Misty. The harder her huffing got, the more I pushed back the sting behind my eyes. She was my best friend. The sun had reached up red and raw in the sky, and I kissed Misty's jaw and told her I'd be back.

Mama and Daddy were throwing a big party this evening, since Daddy's promotion to Head of Sales at the insurance company.

"Rayann, come on, it's noon already." Mama stood in the doorway of my room, hands on her slim hips, get-to-work face on. "You'll sleep the day away, and I need help around here if I'm going to have a party tonight."

I threw the covers off and sat up. "Okay," I said. Since Daddy's new job, things revolved more around him. This time, a party. Since his promotion, he rarely showed up at home before ten at night. Mama would be waiting a dried up dinner. He usually smelled liquory. They'd yell at each other after my brother and I went to bed, our stomachs heavy with gummy rice and gravy.

"I'm up," I said, catching my yawn. I pushed to the bed's edge and curled my dirty toes under so she couldn't spot them.

"You spend too much time with those horses," she said, her back spinned around and headed down the imported Mexican tile steps. She padded across the Persian rug in the TV room towards the kitchen. She hollered orders, I guessed at me, and I only caught parts of what she said. Early on her sighs had swept through the house like the gulf stream winds, prompted by laundry, by Daddy's late business phone calls, by the fact that she realized my brat brother Eric and I were all she'd accomplished in her life. I had decided I'd do anything when I grew up but be a housewife, what every good girl supposedly wished for. I'd raise horses when I grew up. Her strained voice drifted up the stairs and I caught words like clean the ice chest, the crystal, something about arranging the pineapple and cherry centerpiece.

Mama involved herself with the Women's Club, some other housewife organizations and the church circle. And her yard. She had land-scaped it well; the back yard was featured in *Southern Living*.

When she asked me to join the United Daughters of the Confed-eracy, Lily had been in the next room. I felt awkward, like two years earlier when six foot tall Lily was watching Martin Luther King on TV. He and the "Civil Righters" as the news called them, had swum in the "whites only" beaches of St. Augustine, and King had gotten arrested. Lily ironed clothes as she watched TV, one eye always at the front glass door, waiting for Mama to return from errands. I'd looked at her skinny long brown legs and wanted to ask her what she thought. Lily watching other Negroes demand the right to use any bathroom, her ironing our linens and watching the mayhem on TV.

So when Mama had asked about me joining the U.D.C., I'd said No. I could hear Lily shuffling around, polishing Mama's long table by Daddy's chair in the den.

My brother Eric walked into my bedroom, which was right next to mine upstairs. We shared a balcony and a bathroom, and nothing else. He walked up to the bed.

"Get up," he said, bending over so his face got close. "Lazy bones. I've been working all morning, helping for this party. Get up before I tell." Eric never did anything but watch TV and shoot baskets out back. "He's a *boy,* Rayann," Mama had said when I asked why I always washed dishes, swept floors and changed sheets, even his on Saturdays. And Mama bragged about "her boy" to friends. Where he planned to go to college, which position he would play this year on the basketball team.

"You stinking idiot tattletale," I said, standing up on the bed to look down at him. I always felt guilty after I said anything about the way he smelled. But sometimes I blurted before I thought. I acted like Daddy that way. Eric was two years older and stronger, but I could hold my own with him and he knew it. He stepped back a little. "You tell on me," I said, "and I'll brain you." He laughed. "I'll tell them you smoke," I added. It was my only weapon. He twisted my arm and glared at me. "You're a bully," he said. "And you don't act like a girl. You and your stupid horses." All you care about is feeding your fat face, I thought.

"You kids behave, and I don't mean next week, you understand?" Lily said from the bathroom.

I stood up and glared at Eric. He took off out the door. I pulled on the clothes I'd taken off just six hours earlier. I'd hike up to the pasture soon to check on Misty. I could hear Eric downstairs, telling Mama that I'd refused to help again. Mama said something about not having time for this today, and slammed the back door where the terrace stretched from one end of the house to the other.

I ran downstairs and started polishing silver. Eric mumbled, "You stink like a boy," in the kitchen. I pulled back the butter knife as if to stab him. "Do not," I said. I thought of walking Misty around in the dark night, and how she'd stopped and tried to buckle her knees under and drop to the ground. I'd had to pull the nylon rope attached to her red halter, my throat aching and me trying not to sound scared. Misty could tell when I got scared or happy or sad or mad. Even that sick she'd smelled good. "Horses smell cool," I said. Eric left the kitchen making fart noises.

After I finished the silver, I walked outside where Mama threw linen tablecloths across the outside tables. Bleach smells blew through the air as Eric hosed down the terrace with slumped shoulders.

"I have to go check on Misty," I said. You what, Mama said. "She's real sick. The doctor doesn't know if it's colic or worse," I said. "He told me to check on her a lot," I lied. She waved me away and said I needed to get down the crystal, the Waterford, and wash it, and if I didn't she would tell Daddy when he got back from the liquor store, and I knew what that meant, didn't I? I promised I'd be right back.

I cut through the neighbor's front yard to get to the pasture. Buster and Misty, my two horses, usually clomped down to the barbwire fence that separated the pasture from yards. By about one every afternoon, seven days a week, they appeared at the fence, and by three every day they'd have stuck their heads over waiting.

Today they weren't. I slipped between the lines of barbwire and headed through the thicket of trees, up into the pastures to the top of the hill. Just beyond the crest, their water trough faucet dripped a slow dribble.

Buster stood at the top of the hill with his head up high. When he saw me, he started nodding up and down, something he only did when he was really scared. Then I saw Misty. She lay on the ground in the August sun, something a horse never did. Her ribcage heaved up and down.

"What are you doing, Misty?" I said. Her eyes had been rolling around, but when she heard my voice, she lifted her head up. It plopped back down with her heaved breath.

"Come on, girl, stand up," I said. Her fur, usually a dark red, had turned sleek and black from sweat. I pulled at her halter and said, "Please Misty, stand up." She lifted her head; it flopped down.

Daddy and I had driven a horse trailer to Georgia to buy Misty five years before. I rode for an hour before we bought her. The hard quarterhorse trot felt nothing like a show horse. But her canter rocked smoother than Buster's show gait, and she turned quickly to the touch of the bridle. Even-tempered, unlike Buster, who would bite in a bad mood. Misty had never bit once, tried to kick or to run away.

Now I could feel, even hear my kabooming heart like hooves galloping up a dirt road on the outside of my chest. I ran all the way home.

Mama said there was nothing she could do, she was sorry, but I could call the vet again and then get to work on the Waterford. The vet said to give her a few hours and check back with him, but not much he could do at this point. So I pulled down the crystal and washed and swallowed hard. Then I decorated the pineapple in Mama's design, like on of the new round condominiums Daddy had invested in on Panama City beach. Lots of windows. Daddy, please come home soon, I prayed.

Lily's oldest son JT and one of his friends showed up in white jackets to tend bar. Eric had said he didn't want to do it, he might mix the drinks wrong. Mama handed them linen napkins and told the guys to fold them like swans. She showed them. I carried the Waterford glass outside.

"Don't use your hands!" she said. My face turned red and I looked out into her *Southern Living* yard. She instructed him on using the ice tongs as he watched with a blank silent look.

When Daddy returned home, I told him about Misty. He ran his hand through thinning hair and took in a deep breath. He had saved his money for college as a cowhand to go to college, since his family couldn't afford to send him to college. Mama's family money had landed us this house with vaulted ceilings and Spanish antique furnishings.

I could tell by the red of his eyes he'd already been drinking. "Doesn't sound too good," he said. And if I'd wait, he'd go up and check on her with me. But he'd said he'd take us on a picnic to the beach last summer, and never got around to it.

Late afternoon floated in. The car parkers showed up, and Mama told them to light the Tiki torches. "Go upstairs and get a bath and change," she told me. So I sneaked out back to check on Misty. Daddy was asking JT for a drink.

"Now don't forget to use those tongs, boys," he said, joking around. "And don't be taking nips off the bottle, either, or the Mrs. won't be tipping you, if you know what I mean." He chuckled at his own joke. JT and his friend said nothing.

I headed up the pasture. Late summer breeze swayed the tops of tall pines. Everything smelled green, like the new grass where horses bite the pasture down to tender shoots. Misty wasn't moving. I walked over and knelt down to touch her. Cold. Her eyes stared at the sky, small eight balls. No heaving breath. Buster pawed the ground a few feet away. She was dead still. That fast. Dead. Alive one minute, dead the next. I felt numb and cold as the bit on Misty's bridle. I didn't want it to be true.

"No," I said, standing up, my voice shaking. I walked over to Buster and gave him a hug around the chest. He hated those, and usually would give me a bite on the back, but this time he didn't. I couldn't think. Car doors slammed. People talked and laughed down the hill. I walked home on the tar road, sneaked in the back way and headed up to my room to change clothes.

I could hear high pitched laughter in the foyer when my mother met guests, the lilt of her voice that I wished she used on me sometimes as she invited them to have a drink. Women came in with too much Get Set hair spray; the men, hot in their suits, walked straight to the back to get highballs.

I changed into a dress and combed my hair, but didn't bathe or wash my browned hands. They smelled like Misty. I couldn't stand the thought of her lying out in the pasture dead. She needed to be buried. I dragged myself downstairs and waited till Mama finished her conversation with the next guest.

"Mama," I said. She looked at me like, This better be important. "Misty's dead. She's lying up in the pasture. Dead." She took in a deep breath and held it. Then her shoulders stiffened into decision and she let out the breath.

"Honey, there's nothing I can do about it right now." She put her arm around me and said, "Why don't you pass around some of these clam sandwiches, and we'll deal with this in the morning." Like she thought I'd said my Barbie doll's head fell off. Eric passed me and made a face. "You stink," he said, wrinkling up his nose. I walked into the kitchen where Lily stood spreading clam dip onto triangles of white bread.

"What's wrong with you?" she said, spreading dip with her long skinny fingers. "You look like you seen a ghost."

"Misty, my horse . . ." I hesitated, my voice quaking. "She just died up in the pasture. She's lying dead up there in the pasture and nobody'll do anything about it." I told myself, *Don't start up.*

"Rayann, here," she said. Her voice softened as she handed me a crystal platter of white triangles. "Go round with these, ask people do they care for one. Take your mind off things. Can't nobody do nothing right now, here, can they? Now go on. Maybe ask your Daddy what to do."

I walked around like a zombie offering sandwiches while the women stood around the food table talking recipes and fingernail paint. In the back, men talked politics. Would Republicans stay in power in the 1968 election. Daddy was in a pleasant drunk, chuckling, and not arguing politics yet. I went up to him and waited. He didn't notice. I tapped him on the arm.

"What is it, Bet—I mean Rayann?" Sometimes he called me by my mother's name.

"Misty. She died. Up in the pasture, lying on the ground. What should we do?" I said. He stared the way drunk people do, like they're looking at you but not quite looking at you.

"Dead? Are you sure?"

I nodded. "She's not breathing or anything," I said. "Remember? The vet said it could be more serious than colic."

"The vet," he said, standing back up, looking relieved. "Why don't you go call the vet." He turned back to his friend.

The vet agreed it wasn't a good idea to leave a dead horse out in the hot sun on a Saturday afternoon, and he knew somebody who'd come pick her up if we'd fork out fifty dollars. I said Yes without thinking. Mama or Daddy would pay it. I'd lie and tell them the vet insisted we had to do it.

"You having that horse took away in the middle of this party?" Lily said. She'd heard the whole thing. She chuckled. I wanted to say It's not a bit funny. She laughed at weird times. Like when Mama told me I was filthy after I came in from horseback riding and to leave my shoes outside and put my dirty clothes in the washer before I went upstairs. Like Lily had a joke on our family.

"It's not funny, Lily," I said finally. "Nobody cares. Least of all my mother. I'm going up to—I'm going to the pasture, Lily," I said, and slammed the back kitchen door, weaving past a couple of sweaty grown ups talking about life insurance policies and safe real estate investments. I decided to braid colored yarn into Misty's hair for her funeral. I'd seen cowboy movies where the Indians braided their horses' manes for battle. I went around the side of the house to the garage and grabbed red yarn from a box labeled "X-Mas Stuff."

As I walked up the hill, everything looked peaceful. I could hear the party behind me. The world looked bigger, the moon in the afternoon sky. I stared at Misty. So this was what dead looked like. I felt it creep over me. Like passing an accident on the road. I touched her staring eye. It didn't move and felt cool, mushy. I closed that eye and picked up her head and closed the other eye. Her head was heavy. "I'm going to decorate your for your funeral, Misty," I said.

I braided her black mane. It took half an hour. At the end of each braid, I tied a red ribbon. It kept me from bawling. Her fur had turned back to deep red again and had matted up so I ran to the barn down the hill behind the neighbor's house and grabbed a brush, combing her sleek on the one side you could see. Women's laughter came from the house. Buster stood nearby gazing.

I heard a low deep growl and looked around. But it was farther away, down by the party. The truck the vet had sent out to pick Misty up in. He'd said something about the county having a place to bury her. I ran home and saw Daddy, grabbed him and told him somebody was here to pick up Misty's body and take it away. He nodded and I said we had to pay them fifty dollars, and that the truck was out in front. I ran around to the front of the house and saw Mama talking to the guy.

"Where are your shoes, Rayann?" she asked. I looked down at my bare dirty feet. I'd left my good Sunday shoes in the pasture. "And just look at that filthy dress. Did you call this man?" I nodded and lied, told her the vet said we needed to get Misty out of the pasture today. Lucky for me, the truck driver agreed.

"Yes'm. We don't work on Sunday, and you don't want no dead horse lying around for two days in the summer heat." That's when Daddy came out the front and handed the man fifty dollars. Mama told me to go upstairs and change my clothes this instant. I nodded and slipped around the side door. I followed the truck to the top of the pasture, opening the gate for the man.

He backed over to where Misty lay and then turned the growling truck around so the crane end faced her. Some mechanism in the truck let loose two long chains from the crane. The driver told me he'd have to carry her by the legs until he could get to level ground, down to the main dirt road past our drive. I nodded, not understanding. He wound the heavy chains around her ankles, one chain circling her two front legs, one the back ones. He got back in his truck and asked me if I wanted to ride. I shook my head no. Buster had walked away and watched from behind trees.

The man lifted the crane, and Misty's limp legs went up into the air. He lifted it again and up her body went into the air with a jerk, her braids all falling like a black and red cascade down, pointing towards the ground, then springing up and back down. Her body slumped, her ribs stuck out like swords, and I thought they might burst through her skin. I think I screamed. My throat felt like needles. The sound got swallowed by the growling sound of the machine. Misty's head had fallen back, nose pointed towards the ground. I'm sure I'd have heard bones cracking if it hadn't been for the growl. I held the small gate open for him by the neighbor's drive. Misty looked like meat hanging on a hook in the back of the butcher's shop, only larger.

I realized the truck was going to carry Misty right past the party. It did. I ran home and sat in the way back of the yard as the truck grumbled by with Misty swinging limp, the chains starting to pull the skin and fur away so the pink underflesh showed.

Some of the party's people stopped talking. Others curious about the growl, opened the door to the outside to see what the racket was. Mouths hung open. Misty's head swayed from side to side. Some woman said, Oh my god. My father said it was just a dead horse, no need to panic. Then he chuckled nervously. Eric came out, made a face and turned around. Mama never came out.

Lily stood with her hands on her hips, looking like she saw this every day of her life. Then she scanned the party and the back yard with her eyes till she saw me squatting. She beckoned me to come here. I stood up, but the stillness of the moment fused mine and everybody else's eyes on the horse hanging upside down with red ribbons in Misty's braided hair. Like everybody suddenly deep inside remembered something horrible that they couldn't say.

Then it was gone. For a minute there was silence. Then my daddy started talking to some guy about a piece of property he had found on the beach. Prime piece, good investment opportunity, especially with this new condominium concept. Sell to the snowbirds cheaper and more people per square foot.

"More money for the investors, the realtors," he said, "and surely somebody would need some life insurance, too." Then the laughter started up again, and people lined up asking JT and his friend to give them a double. The women walked back inside to admire Mama's pineapple cherry centerpiece and grab another sandwich. I heard the thud of Misty's body hit the truckbed and I jumped. Lily was still standing there looking directly at me, so I walked towards the kitchen.

"Where your shoes, girl?" I told her I'd left them in the pasture. "And look at that dress. Deserve a good licking for that." I stared at the kitchen floor. She wiped her hands on her apron and took my shoulder.

"Something you need to know," she said. "Go on, now. Upstairs," she said. She turned me towards the stairs, pushing me gently up. She started a warm bath.

"Lookahere, Rayann. I ain't gonna baby you. You come on and get in this tub bath, and I'll tell you Mama you got a sick stomach and can't help out. Now come on and do as I say or I'm gonna have to give you a licking my own self."

I peeled off the dirty dress and smelled my browned hands before I sank into the tub.

"You think you the only woman never been heard?" She mopped her forehead with a towel and put the toilet lid down and sat. "You mama, she had this scholarship for a free college education, you know that?"

I'd never thought about my mama going to college. I shook my head no.

"She did. Coulda been a interior decorator. But her own mama wrote her this letter, said, 'You can't be smarter than your husband. You needs to go on and marry that man, forget about that scholarship.'"

"How do you know?" I said. "You aren't in this family." I didn't like her knowing all that.

"Don't matter how I know, doubting Thomas, but if you needs to touch the nail holes in Jesus' hands, well, then you can go find the letter in your mama's underwear drawer. She had it there since I been working here. She takes it out every now and again, look at it. It's about worn out by now."

The warmth of the tub lifted some of the heaviness off me. Still, I didn't like this. I tried to think of Mama wanting something as bad as horses and not getting it. Maybe I could tell her sometime how much I liked the garden—willows and firs, palms and blueberries, ivies and hostas. She'd told me all these names and I hadn't paid any more atten-tion than her to Appaloosa or Arabian. Lily got up and said, "Best get back to it."

"Thanks, Lily," I said. "I been meaning to tell you. You got the most thrilling song voice I ever heard." But I don't think she heard me, headed back down into the noise of the party, spreading clam dip onto triangles of white bread with her long skinny brown fingers.

TWO KINDA FOOLS

The island we live on is not an island but just East Point, this side of St. George's Island where people pay to go across the bridge and vacation. Here on East Point Bay, where the oysters have spoiled and the fishermen can't fish, we have Ards Grocery and trailers and oyster boats with bottoms painted blue. Ards Grocery that offers four ice machines broken out front and a cat painted on the door, a four flat-tired pickup truck with oyster nets that reflect sun's electric eye blue-gray in the May heat.

I'm here at the Shields trailer not owned by the Shields but by Smucker Lee, in the living room trying to fix the wires under the light fixture. Smucker Lee is sixty-nine, has cancer of the esophagus and a chain-smoking habit. He grew up a shrimper's son and says it's too full of risks and he don't like risks.

Neither do I is why I am sweating. The wires are balled up like hair matted and crackling when you touch them, like when you put a comb through your hair in December. I stand on this ladder with a screwdriver feeling like a kite hanging in a thunderstorm air.

Smucker Lee hires me out to help him mow sandy grass lots and fix toy-clogged toilets and listen to trailer renters bellow about how bad Smucker Lee's trailers' conditions are. I get to stay at a shack on the bay with my two daughters in daycare for trade, what used to be Bruce's Seafood and still smells of fish guts.

"Hey, Smucker Lee, turn off the electricity," I say.

"What?" he says. He's deaf from the smoking, but like most deaf from oldness people, he hears what he wants.

"Turn off the current electricity," I say, "the fuse box. Turn it off."

"He don't hurt you none unless you're standing in a bathtub of water," he says, waving me away. Why he calls electricity he, I cannot figure.

I look down off that ladder at the not working fisherman with sea bloated eyes and a snicker like painted on permanent. He's drinking a Busch for breakfast, while Smucker Lee sucks down a breakfast Coke and cigarette. The not working fisherman looks at my butt with shanty eyes, the way out-of-work fishermen look at women's butts here.

A white-hot spark pops in the air. "I don't know, Smucker Lee," I say. Idiots, the not-working beer-bellied fisherman's smile says. I know his wife took the lease on the place, since her employment at the Rock n Shell Shop on the highway that runs beside the bay holds their only steady income.

"See?" I say. "Smucker Lee?" I try to keep the wire ends separate, and they instead are wadded like a bird's nest. My voice is charged up loud. "Switch off the circuit breaker." Smucker Lee walks, not traveling fast but with wheezes, and turns off the living room electricity. He switches it off and still sparks kick through the air. It makes no sense, like all I expect a Smucker Lee house to make.

"How's that light?" Smucker Lee calls at the bottom of the ladder, shining the bulb into my eyes.

"Higher," I yell.

"Only one thing electricity can do," Smucker Lee says. His rasp voice reminds me of crickets and sea breeze mixed up. "He can give you a big scare. See, house current's harmless, unless you're standing in a puddle of water, Shiver."

I'm twenty-six and no fool, and no husband to take over my five- and three-year-old girls if I get zapped. "Turn it off," I say, wiping sweat dripping into my eyes. He shrugs and lights another cigarette, making his way to the main fuse box in the outside heat, mumbling about weak women and shoulda hired a man.

"What a loser," the out-of-work fisherman says, finishing off his beer. "You the manager around here?" He's scaling my on-the-ladder-standing-up self like with an electric eye.

"Kind of. I mow lawns and work around the trailers. Gets me half-off rent." I feel stuck as a car in sugar sand. A life that matters will not flow its way to me except to raise my girls.

"You wouldn't believe the bad wiring in this place," he says.

"Cheap rent," I say, climbing down the ladder.

"It's a damn death trap," he says. He puts out his swollen red fingers. "Name's Eddie Shields."

"Angie Shiver," I say. The unit air conditioner in the living room stops working. "Smucker Lee found the main switch," I say. Eddie smiles at the TV cut off.

"Once I took a job. Almost. As a dishwasher at Myra Jean's Seafood over at Apalachicola. I saw the stuff they washed dishes with. Said 'Corrosive' on the bottle. That dishwasher's hands were red hot and swollen, cuts between fingers. When the manager came through I said something about What if you splatter that corrosive on your dick, will it fall off."

"What happened?" I say.

"I got fired."

Smucker Lee comes back into the house and rummages around in my tool box. "Okay, Shiver, out of the way." He climbs up the ladder like he's volted, stops to hack a cough, and I think he's going to lose balance, tumble to the floor, but he does not. The fisherman goes to the kitchen, and I hear the kiss smack sound of the refrigerator door open and then shut. He comes back, cracking open another beer. A yeasty spray fizzles the air.

"I work as a fisherman," Eddie says. "But the net ban is killing us. I work as a clown on the side."

"A what?"

"You heard me." He sits down on the sofa and paints a stone crab face on. Smucker Lee looks down with a watch-out-for-snakes-in-the-grass look signaled right at me, and I swallow down a crack-up laugh.

"When the Franklin County fair comes through, I hire out as a joker," the fisherman Eddie says.

"Why here?" I say.

"People on vacation, they want a few yuks," Eddie says. "You want to see a picture of me in my get up?"

"Why not?"

Smucker Lee can't get the wires untangled and he's hack coughing again. He climbs down from the ladder. "Can't get the wires untangled. Gonna have to cut and splice." His voice gravel-squawks and he wheezes hard in spurts. He fishes in the tool box, mumbling about tape and old wire.

Out comes a picture in 3-D of Eddie, all dressed up with battery-rust orange wig and jester jump suit, white-faced and leer-red mouth. "Looks great," I say, jiggling the 3-D around to get the zigzag electrified look of it. Eddie the out-of-work clown and fisherman grins.

"You got a husband?" he asks. I shake my head no.

"Two kids, both in day care."

"Found it," Smucker Lee says, handing over the flashlight, battery and hand warmed.

"Smucker Lee, I'll fix it," I say.

"Nah, it's okay. I'll show you the tricks of the trade. I'm what you call an artist at this kinda thing." He lights another cigarette and climbs the ladder. "It's simple," he says, raspy, hacking through the middle of the kilowatted harum-scarum nest of wires. "You just gotta—"

No sparks fly. No wise crack static, no deep-throated boat engine of his nicotine breath. Smucker Lee shudders and drops like an anchor and I catch his bones and barely skin little body in my arms, strong from baby carrying and mower pushing. The tape and wire cutters bounce to the floor and the cigarette sticks to his tongue, blue and hanging out, and his eyes bulge like fishes.

The clown fisherman backs away like a gun got pointed in his face, but he's reaching for the bright orange phone on the kitchen wall.

"We got an electrocution here," he says with a call out for pizza voice.

I lay Smucker Lee down on the sofa, my heart charged up beating, and his eyes close down, the tongue stays stuck, and I pull off the cigarette still burning from his now turning purple tongue. "What do we do?" I say.

"Move," the fisherman clown says, pushing me aside. He blows his big beer air down into Smucker Lee's nicotine chest and makes a fist out of his two fists and hammers down on his bony chested t-shirt. No life-kick comes into Smucker Lee.

"Shit," I say as we both stare down at his stringy body. "Wait," I say, and tear outside to the oyster boat, twenty-three feet long of Smucker Lee's boat sitting in the wild sea oat dunes across the road. I grab the oar and rip back across the road and into the yard and house.

"You gonna *row* him?" the clown says. I don't answer, just stand there deciding. Once, my daddy pulled out drunk Hammerhead Duncan from the Point Bar where he'd taken a fall off the balcony and lay face down in the water, knocked out. I'd watched cause it was a Saturday afternoon when Daddy took me for a Coke. My daddy was the hero, pulling Hammerhead in like a heavy net, pushing his back and then grabbing the closest thing, an oar off a tourist's canoe. He slammed the flat side of the oar on Hammerhead's back till he'd coughed his drunk way back to life.

"You gonna whack him?" the clown says.

"I don't know. It might work," I say. Then I slam down the paddle-end flat-side of the oar with a high voltage whack.

"I ain't believing this," the fisherman clown says. "I am not believing this." I work hard in the July-hot May day in this trailer, sea fog breathing and whacking and wondering if I am breaking any brittle cancerized bones, but trying to blam a switch open in Smucker Lee somewhere. And then the wide gap closes and Smucker Lee's arm circuits jump and flail up and down slices and he coughs a sandpaper-and-phlegm breath and pushes the paddle end of the oar off him.

"Ow," he says, coughing. "What you trying to do, kill me?" I drop the oar with a clatter to the floor and wipe my face on my shirt sleeve and feel dipped in sweat.

"Sorry," I say, panting baked waves of heat off me.

"Hey, this lady saved your life, you should be thanking her," Eddie the clown fisherman says.

"Y'all been fishing?" Smucker Lee says, glancing at the oar on the floor, rubbing at his chest, trying to sit up.

"Take it easy, Smucker Lee," I say. "You've had an accident."

"Accident!" Eddie says, "more like suicide." Smucker Lee has unbuttoned his shirt and looks at the red paddle marks on the skin of his chest. He drops his head back down.

"What happened to my cigarette?" Smucker Lee asks, trying to sit up. Outside the backyard view gives me the scene of a school bus with the windows all busted out.

"I saw a gold spiral staircase, like at the Victoria Inn on St. George only solid gold not brass dipped." Smucker Lee's eyes turn from brown to amber. He screws his head over to me. "Know what I mean?"

"Not really," I say.

"What he's talking about is an out-of-body experience," the clown says. "They had it on Oprah last month."

"I can still see it," Smucker Lee says, staring at the trailer ceiling.

"Oh, yeah?" we both say.

"It's all hazy now," Smucker Lee says.

"What do you remember?" I ask.

"Light. A big tangle of light. Lots of light," he says.

"And?" the clown fisherman says.

"It felt good."

"Did you see anybody?" I ask.

"Nope." The EMT arrives from Apalachicola and walks on in the trailer door.

"He was almost a goner," I say, "but we brought him back."

"I won," Smucker Lee says with a weak fist in the air. Then he starts to hack.

"Right on, Smucker Lee," I say, embarrassed and I don't know why.

The EMT gets the story from Smucker Lee, then takes his vital signs and straps him in to the carry out cot.

"Shiver," he says to me. "Tell Lucinda to keep the fish sticks warm. She'll know what I mean."

"Sure, Smucker Lee," I say. He's been married to Lucinda for fifty-four years, so I figure she does get it.

"I hold the oar tight and want to kneel down with it like King Arthur's sword and put the oar on my knee and sing "Amazing Grace" even though I don't go to church. This oar saved a life.

Eddie the Clown has gotten himself another beer and sits on the sofa, one leg propped up, on the floor.

"Just goes to show you," he says, pulling a long sip off that beer.

"Show what?"

"He saw a light, saw lots of light. Any damn clown could say that." He snickers.

"Hey, this is not a joke." I sit on the sofa, my legs wobbly as a brownout.

"And that paddle routine? I can't wait to try that one on the tourists next winter," he says.

I am staring at him in unbelief. "Zat what clowns do, just make fun of people? Is that it?"

"Hey come on, relax. It's just a joke," he says, waving his swollen red hands and glancing at me.

"He almost died!" I say, holding the oar in an I'll-split-your-sides kinda way.

"Well, he didn't," the clown says, ignoring my stance. "Why'd you let him up on that ladder, messing with them wires, then?"

My tongue acts like it's cut off or drunk.

"They pay us clowns to be fools."

"So. What're you saying?"

"People who take theirself too serious? They're the real clowns," Eddie the clown fisherman says. "The fool does it on purpose."

"You're telling me you got two kinda fools?"

"Your presidents and your congressmen, Smucker Lee. They's the kind runs the world."

I am getting yard hot mad. "So that's why the world's such a mess? Not clowns like stuck-up, making-fun-of people kinda clowns, but clowns like Smucker Lee? Scuse me, I got work to do," I say, picking up the wire cutters and dropping them. Anything like a current from him to me has dissolved.

"Well. Enjoy," he says, lying down with his beer balanced on his chest. I look at those wires and think, It's an electric chair, just forget it. I look at the oar in my hand and point the paddle end at the rest of the wires. For a lightning second I think of my daughters, then they disappear like in the dark on a boat in the ocean where a storm has flashed a bolt nearby. What've I got to lose? A life that does not matter? A life where it pays to be a fool? I feel like I need to prove something to the god of bolts and zaps.

I take aim, careful as a shark. One sharp yank and the nest of wires lets go and spills out like perfect stars floating in a bowlful of ocean.

LOBSTERBOY AND THE TELEVANGELIST

Liza-Pearl and her sisters owned no wings and their short wheelchairing legs could not touch the ground. Their arms and legs flapped like lobster claws, and their family simmered in the freak show pot at the fair south of Orlando, Florida. They stayed in the trailer park, a watery world away from Disney, where, for extra, Lobsterboy thieved from his wheelchair.

If Andrew, the son of Bruce the Televangelist, had wandered to the trailer park first, none of what happened may have happened. Instead, Andrew, desperate, careened himself hell-bent through slanting Florida rain to Pearl City north of the trailer park, searching for a thief; but gritty men beat him limp as a tadpole out of water, stole his money, left him in a side-street puddle.

Later, the gritty men returned to tumble and roll him towards the edge of Lake Oconee that divides Pearl City from the rich side of town. A man jon-boat fishing the lake spied Andrew's fine shoes, picked up the crumpled heap of boy and delivered him across the bluegreen lake until he found Andrew's home.

Andrew's mother, Veronica, paid the fisherman all right and the boy woke long enough to find his sister Lydia blackened by bruises. She told her brother through shrouds of bruises beaten on her that their father the Televangelist had pounded the truth of Andrew's mission out of her. This plummeted her brother into a deep coma.

Lydia came from the unguessable country of Televangelist family. She sizzled inside; then she half-marched, half-stumbled her way to Pearl City, down towards the edge of the trailer park next to the side-show swamp where no boats docked and no boats left the marshy river of clown-blood lipstick, snared tigers and sword swallowers, fat ladies and snake charmers. She announced that her father had turned her out of the house, and she carried no money. She needed a thief, preferably a murderous one. She added that she'd left an envelope with her uncle, the sheriff, and he would open the letter revealing her whereabouts if she did not return home by the next day.

For fun or grief or spite or maybe all three, rat-toothed half-humans gathered around her, their eyes dull and surprised as dead fish gawk. They did not hurt her but one asked, "How come your brother or uncle ain't helped you?" She stood bullet straight, waiting in her bruises and blood scrapes.

They took her to Lobsterboy's trailer, where he sat eye-dart nervy in the living room, waiting.

There were those who paid to see Lobsterboy with his whiskey, his spine-sharp self, his two-pincer stub arms and broomstick legs. His hard-shelled self, half hole-hiding from them with his black pearl eyes.

Lydia walked up the sidewalk. Lobsterboy clacked to the living room door, whisky swilled in his veins, his blood snake-water stagnant.

Liza-Pearl's sisters, fallen upon the Lobsterboy affliction at conception, scurried like the stalked, into the corners of their rooms.

Their mama, JJ, looked at Lydia so hard through her darkened circle eyes and blurred vision that Lydia thought her blind as a seer. Just then a bump-crash.

"Please stop!" Lydia wailed. Her knees had hit the that coffee table she could not see in the dark. Her fear whirled in trailer heat.

"Sit, sit, sit down," Lobsterboy gargled out. She sat.

"Are you the thief?" she asked. He lit the television; the room glowed, phosphorescent.

"You are well connected," Lobsterboy rattled in dark light. "Keep your business in this room." He wanted to know each detail of her crime in mind, of motives, of things to steal, of what Lydia paid.

"I pay well, but my reasons are none of your business," she said. He did not answer so she added, "I need a desperate criminal, one who has no fear and no belief in Christ-our-Savior. I need the worst of people—no one else can do it."

"Switch on the light," Lobsterboy graveled out, and she clicked the light. She took in a lung full of breath.

"Lobsterboy!" she said. His wheelchair and the pincer arms, trembling in the glittery half-light like caged monkeys, reminded her of TV news pictures of him. She remembered him from her child nightmares. She'd heard of his cruelty and drunken huge shows. "He is like Satan himself," her father the televangelist had spit out once. She gathered herself and spoke with college girl clearness.

"The only reason I'm here is extreme urgency," she said, sitting back down on the sofa. "I can't back out. I'll tell you everything. If then you do what I ask, I'll make you rich."

Lobsterboy gurgled and flapped his fin-like claws. She began her story:

A month ago, over breakfast, all had smiled on her family: a televangelist father who had pumped others for money to make him rich. Her father, Bruce, lived in high-church style, gaining his fortune from TV, donating to the church, building a two-story white mansion with columns on Lake Oconee for his wife Veronica, son Andrew and daughter Lydia. He made loans to family and church members at hook-high interest rates to show them, he said, what money was worth.

His kids grew up healthy, honest, careful with money, baptized in the name of Christ-our-Savior, the daughter said.

After breakfast, they had all hugged good-bye, Veronica beginning dinner pies, the children off to university, their father jogging the foggy lake before work. This fine china life would soon splatter to the floor.

The televangelist, on his daily run, spied at the dumpster by McDonald's, a thick leather-bound book, white with gold and red trim, a blue satin ribbon marker. "Holy Bible," it read. He picked it up, brushed off ground-in coffee and ooze of catsup; he glanced around, then hurried back to his home office to study it.

Bruce knew it belonged to Billy Grockett, most famous evangelist on earth. The televangelist held the famous stolen Bible of Billy Grockett. The news of the stolen Bible had hit newspapers, radio, TV. Billy Grockett had owned the Bible since his fifth birthday and guaranteed a reward for its return. The thieves had snagged it with Billy's stereo and computer; here, a thousand miles away, they had dumped it.

Bruce felt lucky, blessed to hold the gilded Bible. The televangelist decided he would keep the sacred charm. He'd hoarded around him treasures of holy missions: the sword of Christ given to him in the Holy Land, a six-foot silver cross from Mexico with Christ hung on it, a wall-length 3-D Jesus at the Last Supper framed, from Memphis. God would blame these as idols, so the televangelist had kept them in hiding so that others would not fall upon false gods. And for beauty he would keep the Bible, he thought.

He told only his first born son, Andrew, what and where he holed up the prize. The son later, to his sorrow, would show this secret, when pushed to it.

At the time, the son thought it spastic that his father sat, trance-like, in his office of idols. So Andrew excused himself, leaving his father in zombied reverie.

The televangelist always sat writing his sermons in the office morning and afternoon, so it wasn't till the housekeeper banged in that afternoon that he was located, and in a trance. Foam padded his lips, his eyes reddened from not blinking, his ears crimsoned. The housekeeper said he looked filled with Christ's blood; it looked as though black blood would any moment seep from his eyes, ears, pores. He had to be helped out of the study; then he exploded.

The whole family had gathered at home, supper time. Bruce shouted at his wife for making the pies with tuna. He hated tuna, he said, the food of peasants like her. Then he picked up the two pies and threw one at Lydia, then one at Andrew.

The televangelist said he despised his wife Veronica, that he'd for eleven years kept a man. In fact, he said he had orgied with teenage boys for years. Already, he'd set up his trust account for the boyfriend, not for his wife; he called his son a wimp, his daughter a slut, and told her she could wear pants no longer, that he had signed her up at a Baptist boarding school.

Then he stumbled to his bedroom, fell fast into the sleep of a baby without worries or guilt, as if with a belly full of milk.

The Televangelist's family shook in the kitchen, arms around each another's arms, sniffling, stunned, uncoiled.

The next morning he woke them all at dawn and forced them to put on the robes of baptism; he dunked them in the bathtub. This he did every morning after. He told them they could see no movies; he ripped up all the books in the library; he commanded them to bring no friends over.

Then it got worse.

At tax time, the televangelist's accountant came over and told him this time, he must pay. Bruce picked up the six-foot silver Jesus cross from Mexico and tried to club the accountant, who tore out of the house.

Then someone who'd made an appointment to get saved by Christ-our-Savior walked into the study to find the televangelist holding the sword of Christ given to him in the Holy Land. The televangelist pointed the sword straight at the sinner's heart; before the televangelist could pull back to strike, the sinner crawled out of the room, ran from the house.

The televangelist struck his wife in the face; his son Andrew jumped his father. His father then punched the son in the ribs and stomach, breaking one of the son's ribs, and consequently his heart. Veronica wept like a blue Mary, begging her husband to get off the son.

"I'll kill you all!" he said, the blood of Christ threatening again to seep to the surface, leaking red tears, oozing scarlet from his ears. Veronica bolted to her bedroom and locked the door. Daughter Lydia, in bold fury, told her father she would not wear dresses only, would not go to the boarding school. His blood-hot strength allowed him to pick her up by the ankles and pitch her outside.

"Get out and stay out!" he said, and he locked the door on her. So Lydia stole into her brother's room and slept under his bed.

The next day, Andrew decided something must be done. He knew what to do.

He stole the Bible from his father's hiding place in the study and told his sister the secret.

"Maybe I'm crazy, Lydia," he said, sitting on his bed where she ate food he'd swiped from the kitchen for her, "but I think this is where the trouble began."

"Get rid of it," she said, massaging her neck, twisted in the fall.

Andrew set out with the Bible to mail it back to Billy Grockett. On the way, he wheeled the garbage can out to the street for pick up, along with the Bible and his briefcase. When he got to the post office, the package had vanished from his briefcase. It was like the Bible had cast a spell on him.

Relieved that the white Bible was gone, Andrew headed home.

When he made it to the lakeside home, he found his sister badly bruised, his mother sobbing wearily.

"What in God's name happened?" he asked. Bruce the televangelist had found the Bible in the trash, his daughter hiding in Andrew's room. The televangelist had pummeled the truth out of Lydia.

"That Bible is a curse on us," Andrew said.

So he went to Pearl City where he had been pummelled and brought back by the fisherman.

"I will do anything to get rid of that Bible," Lydia said. Bruce slept that night on the floor, and as he drifted in and out of the coma, he heard his sister murmur, "I will do anything to get rid of that Bible." In the middle of the night, he woke to her sleeping moans of pain, and her words, a third time: "I will do anything to get rid of that Bible."

The next day, she dressed and said to Andrew, "This must be a genuine robbery, not by someone under the spell of this Bible. But Daddy will be on guard now, I have to plan carefully." Then she limped out the door, crossed through Pearl City and headed down to the trailer park.

"Can you do it?" Lydia said to Lobsterboy. "I mean, how do I know you won't be ruinous scared, spellbound like my brother, who tried to send it back?"

With a leathery creak, Lobsterboy hoisted himself up onto his wheel-chair. His fleshy arthropod arms stuck straight out. They could pummel better than the strong man or the tiger whip. His daughters all knew. Liza-Pearl especially knew, as she threw herself across her sisters to protect them from their father's clapper pummels. With his pincers, he picked up the concrete statue his wife had bought, the six-foot tall pelican and flung it across the room.

"Do you need credentials?" Lobsterboy said, his voice rusty as scrap iron pieces of carny ride.

"Okay," she said. "Okay. My father keeps the Holy Bible under the mattress. But he sleeps sound as a cat and turns sideways during the night, so you should have no problem stealing it. I will give you my mother's whole diamond collection if you can get that cursed Bible out of our house," Lydia's voice wavered on the verge of some awful knowing. "Tonight," she said. "Please do it tonight."

She left, slamming the door, which vibrated through the trailer and into Lobsterboy's daughters. He hacked and coughed, and his wife came and sat in the living room with him. He said he wanted to splish out of the circus and get treatment for emphysema. He was a dying Lobsterboy, and neither he nor his wife were believers. They knew too much of ferris wheel car unlug-nutting, flying out and down, flattening what's in that place, too much to believe in Christ-our-Savior.

He so disbelieved that when his oldest daughter Liza-Pearl had been born, the only child with no deformity, Lobsterboy had immediately crushed her knees so that she would always work the circus.

Lobsterboy and his wife buzzed plans—the three daughters could take the trailer, the wife some diamonds, and with the rest, the two would leave the watery world forever.

That night in the big house on the lake, the televangelist's son Andrew floated in and out of a coma. His wife grew full of grief and stood on the lookout, the daughter waited with the jewels, the father lay asleep. The light by the door in the kitchen downstairs was turned off. Lobsterboy's wheelchair wheel-squeaked over the patio.

A bird sang and blossomed purplish wings; Lydia descended downstairs and opened the door to a bird with lobster claws, and a growling hack. Without sound, the bird flew on wheels up the stairs behind her. At the top of the staircase, they separated, moving apart, towards the hallways of their planned future, not once glancing at each other.

Lobsterboy entered the televangelist's room with professional wheelchair ease. Lobsterboy, the mugger and thief, found that the daughter Lydia had told the truth: the televangelist slept sideways in his bed.

For guilt or fear or sudden sixth sight about his father or all three,

Andrew suddenly woke from his coma screaming: "He's stealing! He's stealing! He's stealing!" Then the televangelist's son fell over dead from a heart attack.

When his mother ran to her son's room and found her son's spirit flung loose and his body chilled, she screamed, waking the televangelist. Lobsterboy was deciding between shuffling himself behind the curtains or choosing a brass candlestick to kill Bruce when the televangelist picked up a .45 he kept in his closet, never noticing the robber. Lobsterboy stole the Holy Bible.

Bruce the televangelist cocked the gun, racing around the hallway, trigger-happy. A shadow ran at him in the hall and Bruce aimed at the heart. He pulled the trigger. He switched on the light. He had killed his wife. He turned the gun on himself. His daughter, Lydia, broke into a confetti of craziness and later had to be dragged to the psychiatric ward by the police.

Lobsterboy knew the plan had unwrapped itself into a blaze of chaos. He climbed out the window with his mighty clappers and crawled himself home. He confessed to his wife of the plan's ruin. He would disappear for a while, he said.

The noise of Lobsterboy's frothing crawl home woke the neighbors who called the sheriff. The sheriff then opened the sealed letter from his niece Lydia. He then released the entire deputy force, homicide squad, volunteers, to the white house with columns by the lake, and to the circus trailer park across town beyond Pearl City.

The sheriff himself shot and killed Lobsterboy, who sat in one of his daughter's wheelchairs in the living room. He fell to the floor, then the Holy Bible fell after him.

The Bible was returned to Billy Grockett. He spouted a speech about the will of God to the congregation, to TV, to newspapers, to magazines. They also all swarmed Lobsterboy's house, and a doctor volunteered to do surgery on the younger sisters, to cut fingers into them and to make them whole.

A miracle occurred; the older daughter, Liza-Pearl, sprouted wings in her knees—she could suddenly walk. The bone chips of her knees had layered themselves together and she walked and walked, the TV crews following closely behind her.

Her sisters, jealous, furious at Liza-Pearl's attention, did not want either a miracle or surgery because they would no longer be able to work at the carnival.

Lobsterboy's wife JJ, with dark undereye circles and dim vision, could suddenly see, and together she and Liza-Pearl walked away from the carnival without one time looking back.

photo of author by Barbie Ryals

A graduate of Florida State University, Mary Jane Ryals grew up in rural northern Florida, where she has lived most of her life. She has a son and daughter, Dylan and Ariel; and her husband Michael Trammell is also a writer. Mary Jane teaches business communications at Florida State. She is working on a novel, presently entitled *How Cookie and Me Got Home*. She has received a grant from the Florida Arts Council and was on University Fellowship for three years. She has also been a recipient of an NEH research grant for her writing.